I0659648

GENDER SWAP
GAMBLER BUNDLE
(Books 1 to 5)
By
Marci Wilcox

ISBN-13: 978-0-9993518-6-4
Copyright 2018 by M. Dubrow.

This is a work of fiction. Names, characters, places and incidents are a product of the author's imagination or have been used fictionally and are not construed as real. Any resemblance to persons, living or dead, actual events, locale or organizations is entirely coincidental. All characters in this story are over the age of eighteen.

No part of this eBook may be reproduced or transmitted in any form or by any means, electronic or mechanical, including photocopying, recording or by an information storage or retrieval system, without written permission from the author.

GENDER SWAP GAMBLER 1

Chapter One

Johnny glanced at his cards before laying them face down on the table. His face showed no emotion. He was so calm that anyone who didn't know him better would have checked to make sure he still had a pulse. Inside, he was doing somersaults and pumping his fist.

Four Queens. This was the hand he'd been waiting for, the one he'd been praying for. It couldn't have come at a better time. He was down to his last dollar. Everything he had was in the pot. If he didn't win this hand, then he was out. Dead broke. No tomorrow. He had to win this hand and then God or whichever saint looks after fools and gamblers came down from the heavens and gave him this winning hand.

From behind his mirrored sunglasses, he peered at the other players through the haze of stale cigar smoke that hung over the table. He'd been losing to them all night. Not because they were better gamblers than him.

His losing streak began long before tonight. But thanks to four sweet Queens, his luck was about to change.

The last bet had been made. It was time for the showdown. Johnny suppressed a smile as he flipped his cards over. He wanted to say something classic like, "Read 'em and weep." But he held his tongue. He would let his four ladies do his talking for him.

He looked at the other players cards. Three of a kind. Two pair. A full house, Jacks high. Four Tens. He had beat them all.

But then he looked at the cards of the man sitting next to him. Five, six, seven, eight, and nine. All hearts. A straight flush. The winning hand.

The four Queens didn't save him after all. Johnny had lost again.

The winner said, "Read 'em and weep!" as he raked in the pot. Johnny fought down the bile that had rose in his throat. If he was going to puke, it wasn't going to be in front of these bastards. He kept his legendary cool as he stood, stretched his aching back, and left the hotel room.

As Johnny rode the elevator down, he prayed for a little bit of luck. Just enough to get him out of the casino without running into anyone he owed money to, which was everybody.

He was still reeling from the agony of getting so close to winning that he wasn't thinking clearly. Otherwise, he wouldn't have taken the elevator. He would have rushed down the twenty flights of stairs to the basement, taken the service entrance to the back alley, sprinted to the parking lot where he'd left his crappy car, and hoped like hell that the engine would turn over. He wouldn't even have stopped at the roach-infested motel where he'd stashed his few earthly belongings. He would have driven as far from Vegas as the car's half tank of gas would take him.

Instead, Johnny got off the elevator and into the all too familiar smell of cheap perfume, cigarette smoke, refrigerated air, and desperation of the casino. All around him people cheered or cursed while retirees unloaded their nest eggs into slot machines one quarter at a time. He hurried across the casino's well-worn carpet toward the exit. He was almost to the open door, the only place where sunlight leaked into the perpetual night of the shiny gambling den, when a gorilla in suit stepped out from the crowd and grabbed Johnny's arm.

He wasn't actually a gorilla. He was bigger and hairier.

"Hey, Johnny," he said. "You aren't leaving us, are you?"

"Hey, Bruno," Johnny said. "I'm just going out for a bite to eat. I'll be right back."

Johnny winced as Bruno squeezed his arm.

"Why go out? We got the best all-you-can buffet."

"That you do, but I'm really craving an In-N-Out cheeseburger and a strawberry shake."

Another casino security guard joined us. Like Bruno, he wore a dark suit and had his I.D. on his breast pocket. He was as big and muscular as Bruno, but Bruno was Italian, and the new guy was African American.

"Hey, Johnny," he said. "You aren't leaving us, are you?"

"Hey, Keith," Johnny said. "I was just explaining Bruno that I'm just running out for a burger and a shake, and then I'm coming right back. You can come with me if you don't believe me."

Johnny was glad that his hoodie hid the sweat stains forming around his underarms. He learned a long time ago to never let anyone see you sweat.

Keith leaned against a slot machine and crossed his arms.

"I heard about the game," Keith said. "On the last hand, you had four Queens and you got beat by a straight flush."

"Damn!" Bruno said. "You sure you can afford that burger and shake?"

"Word gets around fast," Johnny said.

"Yeah," Keith said. "It sure does. Say. If you got a minute, Mr. Jones wants to have a chat with you."

Johnny's legendary cool cracked a little bit at the mention of Mr. Jones. He was the casino manager. The only guy higher up in the casino food chain than him was the owner. Because Johnny had once been a hot shot gambler, the casino had given Johnny a generous line of credit. If Mr. Jones wanted to have a chat with Johnny, it meant the casino now wanted the money that Johnny owed them.

But Johnny didn't have it.

"Sure," Johnny said, as if he had a choice. It's always an honor to speak to Mr. Jones."

Chapter Two

Bruno and Keith flanked Johnny as they led him through the casino. They stopped outside a door with a Staff Only sign. Bruno used his security card to unlock it. Johnny had been escorted through the casino's hidden corridors a few times to visit Mr. Jones' spacious office and remembered the way. But Bruno and Keith didn't take Johnny in that direction.

They led him down a long hallway and through a series of doors until they reached an area of cement floors and cinder block walls. It smelled damp like a cave. They stopped at an industrial elevator. Bruno had to insert a security key and turn it before he could punch the elevator button.

"Are you sure this is the right way?" Johnny said. "I seem to remember that Mr. Jones' office is back that way." Johnny hooked his thumb in the direction they'd come from.

"We're not going to Mr. Jones' office," Keith said.

"Where are we going?"

"You'll find out soon enough."

Johnny held his hands together to keep them from shaking. He was scared shitless, but he wasn't going to give Bruno and Keith the satisfaction of seeing him lose his cool. The elevator arrived. Johnny's legs wouldn't move until Keith gave him a friendly shove.

Bruno pressed the lowest button and they rode in silence to the bottom floor. They exited into a dimly lit hallway. There were two metal doors facing each other. Bruno unlocked the door to the left, pushed it open, and stepped aside.

"Ladies first," he said.

Johnny entered the room. It was pitch-black. He couldn't see a damn thing, but the smell of bodily fluids was overwhelming. It reminded him of a cheap whorehouse he went to when he was a teenager. It wasn't actually a house, but a line of mobile homes. He paid a fat whore to teach him how stick his cock into a pussy.

Bruno flipped the wall switch and the overhead fluorescent lights flickered to live and buzzed like insects. Johnny squinted as he waited for his eyes to adjust. The room's plaster walls had been painted a boring beige and the floor was covered in checkered tiles. It would have looked like a standard storage room except the only items stored inside were two chairs, a small table, and a bed.

The bed was a mattress with no box spring on a steel frame. The mattress looked like it had been rescued from a garbage dump. It had large stains and the stuffing leaked out of large tears on the side. One of the chairs was a comfy looking easy chair. The other chair was an industrial metal chair. It was the metal chair that worried Johnny. It had handcuffs attached to the armrests and front legs. And it was bolted to the floor.

"What the fuck is this shit?" Johnny said, sounding a lot braver than he was.

For two beefy guys, Bruno and Keith moved very quickly. Bruno grabbed Johnny's arms and held him tightly. Johnny squirmed, kicked, and called Bruno's mother all kinds of terrible things as Keith calmly unbuckled Johnny's belt and pulled down the zipper on his jeans. He took off Johnny's lucky Falcons baseball cap and flung it away. He removed Johnny's sneakers and tossed them aside before slipping off his socks. The floor was cold against Johnny's bare feet.

"Now come on, guys," Johnny said. "I support gay rights, but I'm not into man on man action. No offense."

"None taken," Bruno said. "And we're not gay either. Hey, Keith. Need any help getting his pants off?"

"No," Keith said. "I've got it."

Keith dug his fingers into the top of Johnny's jeans and tugged them down to the floor. He did the same with Johnny's underwear. Johnny clenched his butt hole as

11

tightly as he could in anticipation of the men buggering him.

Instead, they removed Johnny's hoodie and T-shirt, leaving him completely naked. Keith piled Johnny's clothes into a corner.

"Shit," Keith said. "I almost forgot these."

He took off Johnny's mirror sunglasses, dropped them on the floor, and crushed them with the heel of his shoe.

Keith and Bruno slammed Johnny into the metal chair and cuffed his hands and ankles. The cold metal of the chair and the cuffs stung his skin.

Johnny struggled against the cuffs, but he was trapped.

"Seriously," he said. "What the fuck is this shit? What are you going to do to me?"

"You'll find out soon enough, bitch," Bruno said as he studied his watch. "Mr. Jones should be here any minute now."

"If you're going to kill me, then please do it quick. I really hate torture."

"Relax girl," Keith said. "You'll find out soon what you can and can't handle."

Johnny hated that they called him feminine words like bitch and girl. It was a sign of their power over him.

Five tense minutes later, the door banged open and Mr. Jones entered with two men behind him. One of the men wore glasses and carried a briefcase. The other one didn't. Bruno dragged the comfy chair across the room and placed it so it was facing Johnny. Mr. Jones settled into the chair and smiled at Johnny.

"You had four Queens and were beat by a straight flush," Mr. Jones said. "Ain't that a bitch. If you had won that hand, we wouldn't be sitting here together."

"Please, Mr. Jones," Johnny. "I'll get you the money I owe you. Just give me a little more time."

Mr. Jones crossed his legs.

"Oh, you're going to get me my money," he said. "And yes, it's going to take time. But on my terms."

Johnny looked at the men standing behind Mr. Jones. They were grinning at him like they couldn't wait to tear into him. He licked his dry lips. Sweat dripped down his sides.

"Please, Mr. Jones," Johnny said. "Don't break my legs. Or any other part of my body. I'll do whatever you want. I swear, I'll make things right."

Mr. Jones chuckled.

"Come on, Johnny," he said. "Give us some credit. This isn't the old days. The casinos aren't run by the mafia anymore. We're legitimate as fuck now. Besides, we learned that it's damn near impossible to get your money back from a guy with busted legs."

Johnny breathed a sigh of relief.

"Thank God," he said.

"I don't know, Johnny. You might wish we had broken your legs."

A chill ran down Johnny's spine

"Why? What are you going to do to me?" he said.

"You haven't met Peter and Logan, have you? Peter's the one in glasses and Logan is the one without glasses."

Peter and Logan nodded at Johnny. He didn't nod back.

"Please, Mr. Jones," Johnny said. "Tell me what you're going to do to me."

"We're living in the age of amazing technology," Mr. Jones said. "And that's how we're going to make you pay back every fucking penny you owe us."

Mr. Jones gestured at Peter. He put the briefcase on the small table. He opened the briefcase, but at an angle where Johnny couldn't see what was inside. He took something out and came toward Johnny. Johnny's eyes widened. Peter was holding a syringe and a vial. He plunged the needle into

15

the vial and drew the liquid into the syringe. Once the vial was empty, squirted a bit of the liquid out of the syringe.

"What are you doing, Mr. Jones?" Johnny said. "What's in that syringe? Are you going to get me hooked on some kind of drug? Are you going to turn me into a junkie and then I'll do anything to get the money to pay you?"

Mr. Jones laughed. The men behind him laughed. Peter shook his head.

"Damn, you have got a wild imagination. I told you, Johnny," Mr. Jones said. "We're using technology. Military grade technology, so advanced the public doesn't even know it exists." Mr. Jones scooted his chair closer to Johnny and leaned toward him. "Here's what happened. A few years back, there was a weapons industry convention in town. You've seen when they've come to town."

"Yeah," Johnny said. "I usually make good money when they're here. Especially when I play poker with the guys from the

Pentagon. Those boys in uniform are all bluster and can't bluff for shit."

Mr. Jones jabbed his finger into Johnny's bare chest. He winced from the pain.

"Exactly," Mr. Jones said. "Couldn't have said it better myself. Those boys in uniform can't bluff for shit. And their budgets are so big, they don't mind losing a ton of money. But then this thing happened a few years back. This general got into a high stakes poker game and lost close to nine hundred grand. Bastard said he couldn't get the cash. He offered to give us some top-secret shit that he claimed was so valuable, we'd be willing to wipe his slate clean. I'll be damn if he wasn't right."

Johnny nodded at the syringe.

"The shit Peter's got in that syringe?" Johnny said.

"It's full of nanny something."

"Nanobots," said Peter.

"That's it," Mr. Jones said. "Nanny something. Gets in the bloodstream. Hell, why should I explain when you can see for yourself. Do it, Peter."

Peter plunged the needle into Johnny's arm. He pressed the plunger down and the liquid entered Johnny's body. At first, Johnny felt nothing. Then he felt a tingling throughout his body. The tingling got warmer and warmer until Johnny felt like his insides were on fire. And that was when Johnny lost his legendary cool.

Chapter Three

Johnny screamed and thrashed about in
the chair. Her screams echoed off the walls.
Tears ran down his face. He strained against
the handcuffs on his wrists and ankles. The
steel cut into his skin and blood ran down his
limbs. But the slicing pain was nothing
compared to what was going on inside his
body. He felt like his internal organs were on
fire. His muscles rippled under his skin and
his bones painfully changed shape.

He shrunk in size. His arms and legs
became slimmer. His skin became softer. His
hips widened and his middle narrowed. His
face changed shape. His hair grew so quickly
it was if it was pouring out of his skull.
Breasts ballooned from his chest. He
screamed in horror as his cock grew smaller.
The smaller it shrank, the higher his voice
rose. His cock disappeared completely into his
body and transformed into a vagina.

Finally, the pain subsided.

Johnny slumped forward. If he hadn't been chained to the chair he would have fallen to the floor. Mr. Jones stood, walked around Johnny, and nodded his approval. He stood behind Johnny's chair, reached around, and grabbed Johnny's breasts.

"Look at the size of these tits," he said. "Who knew Johnny was capable of growing such as fine a pair as these hooters."

He pinched the nipples. Johnny yelped in pain but was surprised that she also felt a jolt of pleasure that traveled all the way down to her new pussy.

"Peter," Mr. Jones said. "Take a picture."

"Right," Peter said.

He took a camera out of the briefcase. He put two fingers under Johnny's chin and tilted her head up. He brushed her hair out of her face. He took two steps back and aimed the camera at her face.

"How about a smile?" Peter said.

"How about you suck my dick," Johnny said.

"And which dick would that be?"

Johnny's eyes widened, and his mouth dropped open. Peter was right. He had no dick. The camera flashed. Johnny could only see spots for a moment. Peter showed Mr. Jones the digital photo.

"It'll do," Mr. Jones. "Send it to the boys so they can get everything ready."

Mr. Jones sat in the comfy chair. He spread his leg out wide and grinned. Johnny could feel him staring at her bare breasts. She blushed and tried to hunch her shoulders together in a useless attempt to hide them.

"Please," Johnny said, her voice soft and meek. "Please don't do this to me. Please give me my dick back. I'm begging you. I'll do anything you want."

Mr. Jones rested his elbows on the armrests and pressed his fingers in a steeple.

"It's a funny thing," he said. "You were such a smart boy. But now you're a dumb bitch. Just goes to show that men are naturally smarter than women. I have no choice but to spell it out for you. I'll turn you back into a man and give you your dick back."

"Thank God!" Johnny said.

"Once you pay back every penny you owe me. Before you start getting any cute ideas, I have no intention of cutting you loose and waiting for that to happen. Until your debt is paid in full, your pretty little ass belongs to me. The casino owns an escort service. You're going to join our stable of whores."

"I don't believe you," Johnny said. "I can see a casino hiring prostitutes, but not owning one of those girl-in-your-room-in-twenty-minutes places."

"Not officially. But then, we don't officially have a way of changing people's gender."

Despair washed over Johnny and she began to sob. Big tears ran down her face. Her cool had dissolved along with her cock.

"I can't believe this is happening to me," she sobbed. "I don't want to be a whore. I want my dick back."

Bruno elbowed Keith's ribs.

"You lose," Bruno said. " I told you she was going to cry. They always cry."

"Damn it," Keith said. "I thought Johnny would keep his cool no matter what."

Keith dug around in his pocket and pulled out a wad of bills. He peeled off a five-dollar bill and handed it to Bruno.

"Don't cry," Mr. Jones said. "I hate it when bitches cry. I understand. You're worried that you won't be a good whore. But I have faith in you Johnny." He stood and looked at his watch. "Well, I've got to get back to work." Mr. Jones headed toward the door. He put his hand on the doorknob and then turned back. "Tell you what, Johnny. Since you're so worried about being a good whore, I'm going to do you a favor. I'm going to have the boys here break you in."

A chill ran down Johnny's spine. She looked frantically from one man to the next. She could see the hunger in their eyes as they gazed at her naked body.

"Something tells me you were going to give me to them whether I cried or not," Johnny said.

"Yeah," Mr. Jones said. "You're right. Turns out becoming a woman didn't make you stupid after all."

Chapter Four

As soon as the metal door clanged shut behind Mr. Jones, the four men began to disrobe. Johnny knew it was useless to plead for mercy. When the men removed their underwear, she peed a little at the sight of their semi-erect cocks. Bruno and Keith were hung like horses, especially Keith whose cock was a long as a baby's arm. Peter and Logan had more normal sized cocks. In fact, Logan's eight-inch cock was very much like Johnny's, when she still had a cock.

Johnny trembled. Images flashed in her mind. Images of cocks forced into her mouth, her pussy, and her ass. She had no way of knowing how painful it was going to be which made the images more frightening and the anticipation more agonizing.

Johnny had never been friends with Bruno and Keith but had never considered them enemies. She wasn't surprised to see that Bruno was as hairy as a baboon or that Keith was a mountain of muscle. Peter and Logan were strangers to her. Peter was pale and flabby. Logan was the shortest and leanest of the four. It was obvious that he was a gym rat. His muscles were well defined, and he had six pack abs.

Logan sauntered over to her and stood in front of her chair.

"We drew straws," he said. "And I won. I get to pop your cherry."

Johnny stared at Logan's erection bobbing inches away from her. A pearl of pre-come hung from the tip.

"You don't have to do this," she said.

"But I want to." He stepped closer to her. "You're going to lean forward and suck my cock. If you don't, I'll beat the living crap out of you. If you bite my cock, I'll beat the living crap out you. If you don't do everything we tell you to do when we tell you to do it, we'll all beat the living crap out of you. Nod if you understand."

Johnny fought back the tears welling in her eyes and nodded. She leaned forward. Logan moved toward her until his cock was pressing against her lips. Johnny opened her mouth. Logan grabbed her hair and shoved his cock into her mouth. She gagged and this time tears did run down her face. He stepped back and she sputtered.

"Is this your first time giving head?" Logan said.

"Yes," Johnny said.

"I heard every gambler eventually had to suck off somebody to pay his debts."

"I guess I've been lucky."

"Until now. Let's try this again. Open your mouth."

Johnny licked her lips and then opened her mouth. Logan went slower this time. He slipped his cock into her mouth. She was surprised at how much it throbbed against her tongue. The musky smell was overpowering. She tried not to think about how his scent was making her nipples hard. He slid his cock in and out of her mouth.

"Work your tongue around it," Logan said. "Ooh yeah. That's good. You're a natural born cocksucker."

Johnny slobbered and sucked Logan's cock. He grunted and groaned with pleasure. He ran his fingers through her long thick hair. She could feel his cock getting harder and warmer. He thrust his hips faster and then grabbed her head and face fucked her, pounding his cock into her mouth. She managed to overcome her gag reflex and allow his cock to ram against the back of her throat. Drool hung from her lower lip. She could hear the voices of the other men echoing off the walls as they cheered Logan on. He held her head close to him so that he was all the way inside her mouth. Her nose was nestled in his pubic hair and his balls pressed against her chin. He kept her there as she choked on his cock. She couldn't breathe and had no way of telling him. Her hands were cuffed so she couldn't push him away. Her fingers flexed helplessly. She began to feel faint.

Logan groaned. Johnny felt his cock twitch as he came. Salty sperm filled her mouth and shot down her throat. She sputtered and did her best to swallow, but his spunk dribbled out the side of her mouth and dripped off her chin onto her tits.

Finally, Logan released her head and pulled out of her mouth. She gasped for air.

"Not bad for your first time," Logan said. "But you still need a lot of practice if you're going to go pro."

Peter took a key ring out of the briefcase and unlocked the handcuffs attached to the armrests and legs of the chair, but didn't remove them from Johnny's wrists and ankles. Bruno grabbed Johnny's arm and pulled her to her feet and gathered her up into his arms. He carried her as if she weighed nothing. He walked over to the bed and dropped her onto the mattress. Peter quickly locked the cuffs on

29

her wrists to the bed frame while Logan did her ankles. Johnny was spread eagle on her back with her pussy exposed.

Peter went back to the briefcase and took out a vibrator. The way he kept taking things out of the briefcase made Johnny think of a magician pulling rabbits out of his hat. He came toward her with the vibrator in his hands. She'd seen this kind of vibrator before. Johnny's ex-wife, Marsha, had one just like it. It was a Hitachi Magic Wand. It was a powerful beast and Johnny had felt slightly jealous of it whenever Marsha masturbated with it. It coaxed titanic orgasms out of her that he could never match.

The men gathered around the bed for the show. They stroked their cocks as they watched. Peter switched the vibrator on. It hummed loudly. He sat on the edge of the bed and rubbed the vibrator's bulbous head against Johnny's pussy. Little earthquakes erupted inside her. This wasn't like anything she'd experienced as a man. If she had been alone, she would have been in heaven. But having four men watch her become aroused made her cheeks burn with shame. She didn't want them to see her have an orgasm, but Peter was pressing the vibrator's head against her clitoris and it was driving her crazy. She squirmed, trying to get away from the magic wand, but it's incessant vibrations overwhelmed her and she began to thrust her hips toward it.

She whimpered and thrashed but the feeling kept building up insider her. The men's erections bobbed around her and her mouth watered with the desire to be filled with a throbbing cock again. Keith and Bruno knelt on either side of the bed. They each took a breast into the mouth. The sucked and chewed on her sensitive nipples.

The combination of sensations coming from her tits and pussy were too much for her to contain. She arched her back and moaned loudly as her first orgasm as a woman rippled through her. Her face flushed and sweat sprouted on her upper lip.

Peter moved the vibrator away from her pussy and slid his fingers inside her sopping pussy. She felt her pussy muscles contract around his fingers. He massaged her G-spot.

"Oh my God," Johnny said as she had her second orgasm. It wasn't as intense as the first, but it made her body craved more orgasms.

"She's good and wet, fellas," Peter said. "Who wants to test drive her pussy first?"

"Me," growled Bruno. "I always thought Johnny was an arrogant fuck who would get his someday. Nothing would make me happier than fucking her brains out."

The bedsprings squeaked as Bruno climbed between Johnny's open legs. He pushed her knees making her legs spread further apart. Johnny stared in horror as he nudged the mushroom head of his enormous cock against her pussy lips. She gritted her teeth and waited helplessly.

Bruno inched his way into her tight wet pussy, stretching her open. At first, it hurt like hell, but even before he was completely inside her, his cock began to feel good. The sensations that spread through her were different from the ones created by the vibrator. The feeling of being filled up was intoxicating and she began to understand why women put up with men.

He squeezed her tits so hard she gasped. He pinched her sore nipples and more tears came to her eyes. She breathed a sigh of relief when he let of her tits. He plopped down on top of her. She was sure he would crush her, but his heavy body felt fine. Every minute, she was learning more about the strength of a woman's body.

She was shocked with Bruno kissed her. He pressed his open mouth on hers and forced his tongue into her mouth. Since kissing is such an intimate act, his tongue was more of a violation of her body than his cock.

She could taste the bologna sandwich he had for lunch.

He reached his hands down and grabbed her ass cheeks as he humped her. She was already wet from the vibrator, but his cock was making her wetter. With each thrust, she opened up more and more until his cock was sliding in and out of her with ease.

"You're such a sweet piece of ass," Bruno said. "I should keep you for myself. Fuck you night and day until you can barely walk. Would you like that? Would you like to be my personal fuck puppet?"

Bruno's musk filled her nostrils. But she also detected another scent, stronger than his. It was earthy and sweet. She realized it was the smell of her pussy oozing juices.

The bed springs squeaked and squeaked as Bruno slammed into her pussy with tremendous force. Her body quivered as drove her toward another orgasm. He squeezed her butt cheeks and screamed as he came inside her. His orgasm released hers and

Johnny bit her lower lip as the orgasm ripped through her.

Bruno climbed off of her, leaving her covered in both her sweat and his. Her head rolled to the side. She could see Keith sitting in the comfy chair slowly stroking his long black cock. He winked at her.

"Don't worry," he said. "You won't have to wait for this much longer."

Johnny shuddered at the thought of that horse cock inside her. Peter sat on the bed, blocking Keith from her sight. He positioned himself so that she could suck his cock with her head turned to the side. He wasn't as urgent as Logan had been, so he was easier to handle. While she gave him a blow job, she felt someone between her legs. She peered down as best she could with Peter fucking her mouth and caught a glimpse of Logan.

She felt his fingers playing with her clitoris. The combination of him finger fucking her and Peter face fucking her was sending sensations in all directions of her body. Then Logan's fingers slipped out of her and a moment later, she felt his tongue licking around her pussy lips.

"Dude!" Bruno said. "If you wanted to taste my dick, then you could have just blown me."

Logan ignored Bruno and continued to nibble and tease Johnny's pussy. He stuck his fingers insider her as he sucked on her clitoris. Johnny moaned and sucked harder on Peter's cock. The two men continued their combined assault on her body until she climaxed again. She couldn't believe her body could handle so many orgasms. Peter pulled out his cock and jerked on it. He groaned as he came. Long ropey streams of sperm splattered on her tits.

The two men got off the bed. Johnny stared at the ceiling as she tried to catch her breathe. She was exhausted. Her arms and legs ached from being stretched out. She felt a cool puddle of sperm and pussy juices under her ass. She wanted to sleep and sleep and wake up to find that this whole thing had been a terrible nightmare.

Instead, she saw Keith's humongous cock loom over her.

"Take the cuffs off her," Keith said. "She ain't going nowhere."

Peter took off the handcuffs. Johnny rubbed where the metal had sliced into her skin. She raised herself up on one arm and gazed up at Keith.

"Please," she said meekly. "I can't take anymore."

"Girl," Keith said. "You ain't even got started yet. Get on your hands and knees. I'm going to break you in right."

Johnny's lower lip quivered as she got on her hands and knees. The bedsprings complained as Keith's heavy body got on the mattress behind her.

"Lower you head down and stick your ass higher," he said.

Johnny did as he instructed. She felt even more exposed than when she had been spread eagle. She felt the heat of Keith's body as he positioned himself behind her. She felt the head of his cock pressed against her swollen pussy lips. She could smell his cologne as he began to enter her.

She gasped. It felt like a log had been jammed inside her.

"Calm down, girl," Keith said. "I'm only halfway in."

Johnny grabbed the edge of the mattress as Keith forced the rest of his cock inside her. She felt like she was being ripped apart. He grabbed her hip with one hand and placed his other hand between her butt checks. As he slid in and out of her, he forced his thumb into her asshole.

Holding her hip and her ass, he pounded into her. Her face was pressed into the rank mattress. He grunted like an animal as fucked her faster and faster. She could hear the men chanting, "Keith, Keith, Keith." She had a series of violent orgasms. Something inside her broke and she begged him to never stop fucking her.

She didn't even notice when he came. She was too far gone. He pulled out and she slid down onto her stomach with his come leaking out of her pussy.

Ten minutes later, the men took turns fucking her again.

An hour later, the men were all dressed except for Keith. He sat in the comfy chair while Johnny was on her knees between his legs. She sucked on his balls while slowly stroking his cock. Occasionally, Keith patted her head affectionately.

Peter took out his cellphone and called Mr. Jones.

"She's ready, sir," he said.

Chapter Five

At midnight, the van pulled into the motel's parking lot and parked in front of room number thirteen. The curtains on the other rooms were pulled aside to spy on the new arrival. Logan was driving. Peter was in the passenger seat. Johnny was alone in the back. Her already sore ass hurt even worse after bouncing around on the van's hard metal floor. Logan turned the headlights off but kept the engine running. Peter got out and opened the back doors.

"Get out," he said.

Johnny climbed out of the van.

She wore her T-shirt, hoodie, and socks. The rest of her clothes, including her wallet and her lucky baseball cap, had been stuffed into a plastic bag and taken away. Peter had explained that the clothes no longer fit her, and she wouldn't need her wallet. He promised that the casino would keep her things in a safe place and that she'd get them back after she'd earn the money she owed Mr. Jones.

With her new reduced size, the T-shirt came down almost to her knees and the hoodie threatened to swallow her up. The sleeves hung over her hands and when she hugged herself for warmth, she felt like she was wearing a straitjacket.

Johnny kept her head down as she followed Peter to room thirteen. Whatever pride or fight she'd had in her had been fucked out of her in the basement. Peter fished the room key out of his pocket and unlocked the door. Johnny followed him into the room.

The room was so narrow they had to walk in single file. It had all the basics, a bed, nightstand, closet, desk, and chair. In an alcove was a bathroom sink. In the corner of the alcove was a mini-fridge and on top of the fridge was a microwave. A door in the alcove led to the shower and toilet.

Peter put the room key on the desk next to a pink handbag.

"Welcome to your new home," Peter said.

Compared to the roach infested crappy hotel that Johnny had been living in, this was a fucking palace. Everything was clean. Even the bedsheets looked like they'd seen the inside of a washing machine in the past week and though it was an old motel, it was clear that the entire place had been recently renovated. She bet it even had hot water and was eager to find out if did.

"Before I go, we need to go over a few rules," Peter said. "The first and most important rule. Get the money before the sex. I repeat- money before sex. Guys will try to rip you off if you don't. I bet you were the kind of guy who ripped off whores."

Johnny sat on the bed and stared at her dirty socks.

"Second rule," Peter continued. "Don't fuck anybody for free. That includes hand jobs and blowjobs. If someone like Bruno or Keith comes sniffing around here and tries to convince you that since you both work for Mr. Jones then they're entitled to a freebie, tell them they have to pay like all the other customers. Your pussy and your mouth belong to Mr. Jones and he doesn't give anybody a free ride."

Johnny nodded to show that she was listening.

"Third rule," Peter said. "No gambling of any kind. Not even one fucking quarter in a slot machine. We don't care if you play cards with the other whores for shit like tampons and lipstick, but never for money. Under any circumstances. You already owe Mr. Jones enough money. We don't need you adding to it. We understand that you're a gambler and that this will be the hardest rule of all to follow. So, Mr. Jones told me to make sure you were aware of the consequences if you break the third rule."

Peter reached into his jacket and pulled out a handgun. He held the nuzzle against Johnny's head. Johnny whimpered and held her hands up in surrender. Her hands shook and her heart beat against her chest.

"You break the third rule and we put a bullet in your head," Peter said. "Do you understand?"

"Yes," Johnny said. "If I break the third rule I get a bullet in the head."

"Good girl." Peter put his gun away. "You'd better get some sleep. You start your new job tomorrow."

Peter left the motel room. Johnny went to the window and pulled aside the curtain to peek out. She watched the van back up and drive away. Then she sat on the bed and cried.

After she'd had a good cry, she stripped off the T-shirt and hoodie and went into the bathroom. She sat on the toilet and peed. This sitting down to pee thing was something she was going to have to get used to.

She was relieved to see that there were clean fluffy towels, soap, and shampoo. She went to the shower and turned on the hot water. Soon, steam was rising. She was right. The hot water did work.

She had sperm in her hair, caked on her face, tits, ass, and inner thighs. Her pussy had a sour smell from all the sperm ejaculated inside her. She prayed that her new female body didn't come with a functioning uterus.

She got under the hot water and let it wash away the spunk on her dirty body and the tension in her shoulders. She shampooed her hair. She wanted to explore her new body, but it was so sore she could barely touch it. She gently scrubbed it clean.

When she finally got out, the room was covered in steam. She dried herself with a towel and then wrapped it around herself the way she'd seen Marsha do it so that it covered her from her breasts on down. She would have wrapped her hair but didn't feel ready for anything that advanced.

She went into the main room. There was a dressing mirror mounted to the wall. Johnny stopped to look at herself. She hadn't actually had a chance to see what she'd become. She took off the towel and stood nude in front of the mirror.

She couldn't begin to explain how bizarre it was to not see Johnny the man. She knew the person in the mirror was her, but really, this woman was a stranger. She peered a little closer. The eyes hadn't changed. She still had Johnny the man's eyes.

Johnny was surprised to see how attractive she was. She had long dark hair, a cute button nose, and full lips. Her breasts were big but not humongous. Her stomach was flat, her legs were smooth and shapely. She turned to look at her ass. It was a mighty fine ass. If she had seen this girl when she was still a man, she would have hit on her big time.

Even though it was sore, she touched her pussy. She found her clit and rubbed it gently.

She felt a tingling in her stomach. With her other hand, she pinched her pink nipple. She thought about the men's cocks. Their big hairy smelly erect cocks. She could still taste their salty sperm in her mouth. She yearned for another meat injection.

Goddamn Mr. Jones. He understood gamblers too well. They had addictive personalities. Johnny was addicted to gambling. His fingers ached for the feel of cards in his hands when he was away from the game for too long. He hungered for the thrill of the game, reading the other players, fooling them into believing his bluffs, seeing his pile of chips grow as he eagerly waited for the dealer to begin a new hand.

Mr. Jones had done more than turn Johnny into a woman. He made sure to get her addicted to cock the same way Johnny was addicted to poker. She'd make him a pile of money as she feed her new addiction.

Johnny put her T-shirt back on and searched the room. There was nothing in the closet or under the bed. There wasn't a phone, a TV, or even a Gideon's bible. There was nothing in the mini-fridge.

She ended her search by going to the desk and picking up the pink purse. She'd noticed it the second she and Peter had entered the motel room. It was impossible to miss it since it was the only personal item in sight in an otherwise empty room.

She opened the purse. Inside she found a hairbrush, lipstick, eyeliner, blush, Tic Tacs, condoms, an energy bar, and a pink wallet. In the wallet, she found a crisp twenty-dollar bill and a driver's license.

Johnny took a deep breath before she looked at the license. The photo was of her. She appeared shocked. This must be the photo Peter took of her when she was cuffed to the chair. The birth date was Johnny's birth date. She didn't recognize the address. She also didn't recognize the name. This was a license for Jenni Jones.

Becoming a woman didn't make Johnny stupid. She understood what they had done. The casino had put Johnny in a plastic bag and were keeping his manhood in a safe place until his debt was paid. And until that debt was paid, she would be Jenni Jones. The last name Jones was a reminder that she belonged to Mr. Jones.

Jenni put the driver's license back in the pink wallet and put the wallet back into the pink purse. She turned out the lights and got into bed. Though she was exhausted, she couldn't sleep. She stared at the ceiling.

She swore that she wouldn't stay Jenni forever. She would kick her new addiction to cock. She'd pay back Mr. Jones and get her own cock back. She'd be Johnny again. That was rule number four. Become Johnny again.

The End

GENDER SWAP GAMBLER 2

Chapter One

Rap! Rap! Rap!

"Go way," Jenni mumbled into the pillow.

Rap! Rap! Rap!

"Clean room later."

Rap! Rap! Rap!

Jenni rolled onto her back and opened her eyes. She grabbed her breasts. Shit. She was still a woman.

Rap! Rap! Rap!

"Coming!"

She threw back the covers and climbed out of bed. She yawned and scratched her ass as she ambled toward the door. She peeped through the peephole. A petite Asian woman was outside tapping her foot. Jenni cracked open the door.

"What do you want?" Jenni said.

"I'm selling Girl Scout Cookies," the woman said. "What the fuck do you think I want? I want to come in."

Jenni narrowed her eyes at the little woman. She looked pretty fierce. It was too early in the morning for a confrontation. Jenni didn't see any harm in letting the woman in. She had nothing to steal. She opened the door the rest of the way and stepped aside so the woman could enter. She came in and sat on the desk. Jenni sat on the bed facing her.

Jenni noticed the woman had an oversized purse and a large blue IKEA bag. She placed the purse on the desk and the bag at her feet. Maybe she had Girl Scout Cookies after all. The thought of cookies made Jenni's stomach grumble. The last time she had something to eat she was still a man.

"I'm Lucy," the woman said. "I'm sort of the den mother for all the ladies living here. I do my best to look out for my girls."

Lucy held out her hand. She had gaudy rings on her first three fingers. Jenni shook her hand.

"Am I supposed to be one of your girls?" Jenni said.

Lucy put her hand on Jenni's knee.

"I know today your name is Jenni and yesterday it was Johnny," Lucy said. "I work for Mr. Jones same as you. Officially, we're both his girls."

Jenni felt a chill run down her spine. There was something familiar about Lucy, but she couldn't put her finger on it.

"Have we met before?" Jenni said.

"We have."

"When?"

"It'll come to you." Lucy opened the IKEA bag. It was stuffed full of packages. She rifled through them and pulled some out. "I'm guessing that T-shirt you're wearing is the only item of clothing you have right now."

"I also have a pair of socks and a hoodie."

"In other words, you have nothing to wear. I'm going to take you shopping, but you're going to need to something to wear to the store. Isn't it ironic that you need clothes to go clothes shopping?"

53

Lucy laid the packages she selected on the desk. Jenni stood next to the desk with her arms crossed under her breasts. There was a pack of cotton panties in various colors, a pack of women's tank tops in various colors, a pair of yoga pants. and flip flops.

"These are all mediums," Lucy said. "But if they don't fit, I have large and small too. I didn't bring any bras because I don't have your size yet. I figured you can go braless for now."

"Thanks," Jenni said.

"Don't thank me. Thank Mr. Jones."

Lucy snapped open her purse, rummaged about, and took out a tailor measuring tape, a pad of paper, and a pen.

"Take you T-shirt off," Lucy said. "I need to take your measurements."

Jenni put her hands on her hips.

"Why can't you take them over my T-shirt."

Lucy rolled her eyes.

"For fuck's sake. You don't have anything I don't have."

Reluctantly, Jenni grabbed the hem of the T-shirt and pulled it off. Though men had already seen her naked, she still felt odd being nude in front of Lucy.

Lucy wrapped the tape measure around below Jenni's breasts and then around them. She measured Jenni's waist, her height, her inseam, and even her feet. She jotted down each number in her notebook. Once she was done, Jenni quickly put the T-shirt back on.

"This is very impressive," Lucy said.

"Really?" Jenni said. "What's the damage?"

"Your 5'8", your shoe size is 9, and your bra size is 32DD. Your measurements are 37-25-36."

"Damn. I'd fuck me."

"So, would I. In fact, I want to right now."

"What?"

Lucy stood and put her hands on her hips.

"I'm serious. I want to eat your pussy right now. Afterwards, we'll get breakfast before we go shopping."

Jenni's eyes widened. Peter had told her that she would start work today, but she never imagined that her first customer would be her "den mother."

"Um...okay," Jenni said. "But Peter was very clear about the rules."

"I know," Lucy said. "Rule number one. Money before sex."

Lucy took her wallet out of her purse and took out three one hundred dollar bills. She folded them over and handed them to Jenni. Jenni opened her pink purse and put the money in her pink wallet. She couldn't believe it. She'd accepted money for sex for the first time. She was officially a prostitute.

"Before we do this," Jenni said. "I need to pee."

"Yeah, me too," Lucy said. "You go first."

Jenni went into the bathroom and shut the door. She sat on the toilet and emptied her bladder. She had butterflies in her stomach. She felt like she was about to have sex with a girl she picked up in a bar. Lucy certainly looked like the kind of woman Johnny would have picked up in a bar.

Jenni wiped her pussy when she was done and flushed. When she came out, Lucy was removing her clothes. She was down to her bra and panties.

"Thank God," Lucy said. "I had way too much coffee this morning. I thought I was going to pee in my pants."

Lucy dashed into the bathroom. Jenni could hear her urine splashing into the bowl through the closed door.

"For what I paid you, you'd better be naked and on the bed when I get out," Lucy shouted.

Jenni stripped off the T-shirt. She sniffed it. She noticed that she had a new scent now. A female scent. There was still a trace of a male scent in the fabric, a little bit of Johnny that hadn't completely disappeared.

She got on the bed and leaned her head against the pillow. Jenni wondered where had she met Lucy before. They must have both been men at the time. Jenni thought about the room where Mr. Jones had Johnny turned into a woman. It stank of fear and sex. Of men and women. Johnny hadn't been the first gambler to pay his gambling debts with his gender.

Jenni wondered how many call girls were former gamblers. The gambling life is hardly a stable life. It's common for gamblers to disappear for months at a time. Nobody was looking for Johnny.

Along with wondering how many debt-ridden gamblers were victims of Mr. Jones' top secret military gender changing nanobots, Jenni also wondered for how long this had been going on? If she knew that, she'd get a better idea of how long she'd have to remain a woman before she could buy her gender back.

The toilet flushed and Lucy came out of the bathroom. She had taken off her bra and panties. Jenni desperately wished she still had her cock. She would have loved to fuck this woman.

Lucy had shoulder length black hair, almond shaped eyes, full lips, smallish pert breasts with big brown nipples. She had shaved her pubic hair into a neat landing strip. She was thin but still shapely. Tight was the word that came to mind. Her body was very tight. Best of all, she had spent time in the sun so that she had nice tan lines around her breasts and pussy where the skin was light brown and the rest of her was a darker shade.

She climbed between Jenni's legs. She flicked her tongue along Jenni's slit, sending wonderful sensations through Jenni's body. After having four guys slam their cocks into her repeatedly the day before, having a woman eat her out was a pleasant change. Lucy knew just how to use her tongue to tease Jenni to a glorious orgasm.

But Lucy wasn't satisfied with giving Jenni just one orgasm. She continued to nibble and lick while she inserted her fingers into Jenni and teased her G-spot. Jenni felt a warmth in her stomach spread out to her nipples and toes. She pinched her nipples as she built up to an even bigger orgasm. She arched her back and moaned loudly as she came.

Lucy sat up with a shit-eating grin, her face was wet with Jenni's ejaculate. Jenni couldn't believe that Lucy had paid her to get her off.

"Is there anything you want me to do to you?" Jenni said.

"No, I'm good," Lucy said. "Besides, you can't afford me."

Jenni laughed. She didn't think she'd ever laugh again. While Lucy washed her face in the sink and reapplied her make-up, Jenni took a shower. After the shower, Jenni got dressed. She found that the mediums worked.

As she slipped on a pair of light blue cotton panties, Jenni realized this was the first time she was putting on women's clothing. Somehow, this made her feel more like a woman than having a penis enter her vagina. She was used to men's clothes that hung on the body loosely. Women's clothing clung to the body and were softer than men's clothing.

Once she was dressed in black yoga pants, a red tank top, and orange flip flops, she looked at herself in the mirror. She wasn't happy with how her nipples made indentions in the tank top or how colorful the outfit was, but at least she body was covered enough so that she could go out into the world.

Out into the world. This would be her first excursion into the city as a woman. She gasped. She couldn't catch her breath. Lucy put her arm around Jenni's waist.

"It's okay," Lucy said. "You're just having a mild panic attack. It happens to all of us the

first time we have to go out to where
everyone will see us. Just remember. Nobody
but us knows that you were ever anybody else.
As far as they know, you've always been Jenni
Jones."

Jenni shut her eyes and took deep
breaths. She nodded at Lucy.

"Thanks," she said. "I'm better now."

"Good," Lucy said. "Let's go shopping."

Chapter Two

Jenni and Lucy lay in bed on their backs, side by side, and stared at the ceiling.

"Being a woman is exhausting," Jenni said.

"It does take some getting used to," Lucy said.

Lucy and Jenni had gone to the Eastern Indoor Swap meet to get Jenni everyday clothes and shoes and then to Showgirl Supplies for work clothes and shoes. In Jenni's opinion, the clothes Lucy chose for her from Showgirl Supplies were slightly sluttier than the everyday clothes she chose for her at the flea market.

Jenni thought that was it for the day, but Lucy explained that they were just getting started. She took Jenni to a nail salon for a manicure and a pedicure followed by having her nails and toenails painted with red nail polish.

Next, they went to a beauty salon where Jenni was subjected to a facial, an eyebrow threading, and a lip wax. At first, Jenni refused to get a bikini wax. She wanted to keep her pubic hair naturally bushy exactly as God had intended it to be. But Lucy insisted Jenni have it removed for professional reasons. Men (better known as customers) were so used to trimmed bushes or better yet, a bare pussy, that pubic hair now grossed them out. The procedure was the most painful thing Jenni had ever experienced and her crotch still felt like it was on fire. After all those humiliating and painful procedures, getting her hair cut and styled was relaxing. Jenni just wished they'd had something else to read other than women's fashion magazines while she was getting her hair done.

When they left the salon, Jenni thought sure they were done, but Lucy had one more stop. They went to a tattoo and piercing parlor to get Jenni's ears pierced.

"That's a bit permanent," Jenni said.

"You can always let the skin grow back later," Lucy said. "Come on. All women wear earrings. It'll look weird if you don't."

Reluctantly, Jenni went into the parlor. A man covered in tattoos iced Jenni's earlobes before piercing them. There was a quick sharp pain followed by a longer dull pain. Lucy gave the man a pair of diamond stud earrings to put in Jenni's ears.

"I can't accept those," Jenni said.

"Don't worry," Lucy said. "They're not real diamonds."

Somewhere in between all that running around, they had stopped at a Denny's to eat. Jenni was starving and ordered a big meal, the kind she was used to eating as Johnny. But she couldn't even finish half of it. She wondered if it was because her stomach was smaller now.

When they got back to Jenni's room, Lucy taught her how to shave her legs, how to put on a bra, how to select the correct make-up for her skin tone, and how to properly take care of her hair. Lucy was surprised that she didn't need to show Jenni how to put on make-up and lipstick.

"I spent half my married life waiting for Marsha to put on her war paint," Jenni said. "I started watching her to see why it took her so damn long."

Finally, Lucy helped Jenni pick out what to wear for her first night as a call girl. Jenni was sure she'd select something super slutty, but was relieved when she handed her a simple black dress.

"This is a V-cut mid sleeve party dress," Lucy said. "You want something that says hey I'm available to the client without screaming hey I'm a prostitute to the cops. Wear it with your black fuck me pumps."

Jenni tried the clothes and the shoes on and looked at herself in the mirror. When she had looked at herself earlier in the mirror, she had to admit that she made an attractive woman. But now that she was all dressed up with make-up and her hair done, she had to admit that she was fucking hot!

The dress hugged her curves and was just low cut enough to fire up a man's imagination. The heels had a way of making her ass look ever better than it already did. She put her hand on her hip and thrust her chest out. She stuck her finger in her mouth and tried out a come-hither look. She couldn't believe it was her.

"What do you think?" Jenni said. "Am I a sexy bitch or what?"

Lucy answered Jenni's question by pushing her onto the bed, lifting up her skirt, yanking down her panties, and licking her pussy until she had a screaming orgasm.

Afterwards, the exhausting day caught up with them and the two women could barely move. The bed felt so good and Jenni was tempted to drift off to sleep. She nudged Lucy.

"I know who you are," Jenni said. "Or rather who you used to be."

"And who I will be again once I pay off my debt," Lucy said. "Tell me. Who do you think I am?"

"Luke Lee."

Lucy sat up and peered at Jenni.

"How did you figure it out?"

"You know how poker games can go on for hours. Days even. You get to know the other players. All that time to shoot the shit. Some of the talk gets personal. Almost like we're in a therapy session. On more than one occasion, you talked about how much you liked going down on girls. You said you loved eating pussy more than fucking. It dawned on me while you were eating me out that you were Luke Lee."

Lucy put her first two finger in a V around her mouth, stuck her tongue out between them, and wiggled her tongue.

"That's been the one good thing about having a pussy," she said. "I've learned to be even better at it than I was before and I was the best."

Jenni's pussy tingled as she thought back to the orgasm Lucy coaxed out of her in this very bed that morning.

Rap! Rap! Rap!

Jenni stared at the door.

"Who the hell could that be?" Jenni said. "I know it's not you this time."

Lucy glanced at her watch.

"Sorry girlfriend," she said. "It's time for you to go to work."

Jenni sighed. She'd almost forgotten what all this girly dress-up was for. She slid out of bed and opened the door. Logan stood outside. He wore a dark suit and mirror sunglasses.

"I just need to put on my shoes and then I'll be ready to go," Jenni said.

She put on the black fuck me pumps and grabbed her pink purse. Lucy gave her a hug and a kiss on the cheek for luck and then Jenni was out of the room. She shivered both from nerves and the cool wind on her bare legs. From the motel's parking lot, Jenni could see the Luxor's pyramid on the other side of the Las Vegas Freeway. The late afternoon sun glinted off the hotel's windows.

Logan wasn't driving a van this time. He'd come in a sleek town car. Jenni was about to get in the passenger seat when Logan told her to get in the back. Logan slid in behind the wheel. He twisted around in the seat.

"Here," he said. "You'll need these." He handed her a burner phone and a wristwatch. "From now on we'll call you on that phone when you have a client. Don't use it for anything else. You work by the hour so use the watch to keep track of the time."

Jenni put the phone in her purse and the watch on her wrist. Logan started the car and pulled out of the parking lot. Soon, they were on the freeway headed toward the strip. Jenni felt small and helpless sitting alone in the big back seat. She sniffed back tears. She didn't want to mess up her make-up. Logan glanced at her in the rear-view mirror.

"First day on the job jitters?" he said. "Don't worry. All you have to do is spread your legs and let the man do all the work."

Chapter Three

Jenni wobbled through the lobby of the MGM Grand. She hadn't had time to master walking in heels and worried that she might fall on her ass at any moment. The short dress made her feel exposed and she was sure everyone was staring at her.

"Calm down," she said, taking a deep breath. "You're just another face in the crowd."

A man in a Hawaiian shirt and cargo shorts stepped in front of her. She didn't need to smell his breath to know he was three sheets to the wind.

"Hey, baby," he said. "Don't look so sad. Give me a smile."

"Fuck off," Jenni said.

She tried to walk past him, but the man grabbed her arm.

"You don't have to be such a bitch," he said. "I was just trying to be nice."

"Please let go of my arm," Jenni said.

People looked the other way as they hurried pass her and the obnoxious drunk. He was taller than her and probably outweighed her by a hundred pounds. If she were still a man, she would have kicked his ass. If she were still a man, he wouldn't be bothering her.

With his free hand, the man reached into his pocket and came out with a wrinkled five-dollar bill. He waved in Jenni's face.

"I'll give you five dollars if you let me feel your tits," he said.

"What?" Jenni said.

She tried to pull away, but he held on tightly.

"I just want to see if they're real."

Jenni wanted to scream for help, but she couldn't. She was a prostitute on her way to see a customer. She didn't dare call attention to herself. Maybe if she let the drunk feel her tits, he'd let her go. But then that might encourage him to do something worse and cause her harm.

"Is this man bothering you?"

Relief poured through Jenni. A beefy security guard had come to her rescue.

"I'm just trying to have a friendly conversation with this pretty young thing," the drunk said. "But she's giving me nothing but attitude."

"I wasn't talking to you, sir," the guard said.

"Yes, he's bothering me," Jenni said. "He won't let go of my arm."

"Sir, let go of the woman's arm."

The drunk glared at the guard and then at Jenni. He let go of her arm.

"I don't know why you're taking the whore's side," he said.

"Excuse me?" the guard said.

The drunk gestured at Jenni.

"Just look at her. It's obvious she's here to fuck somebody. For money. That's what whores do."

The drunk jammed the five-dollar bill into Jenni's cleavage.

"Now will you let squeeze your tits?" he said.

The guard grabbed the drunk's arm.

"I'm going to give you a chance to walk out of here on your own two feet provided you go right now," he said. "If you don't, then I will pick up your sorry ass and toss you out onto the street."

"But I'm staying at this hotel," the drunk whined.

"You just checked out. I'll make sure your bags are delivered to the front of the hotel."

The drunk squinted as he swayed back and forth.

"Fuck it," he said.

He ambled out of the hotel. The guard faced Jenni. Her cheeks burned with embarrassment. She pulled the five out of her cleavage, crumpled it up, and squeezed it in her fist. Her chest ached where the man had stuffed the money.

"Thank you," she said.

"Just doing my job, ma'am," he said. "Where were you headed before that jerk assaulted you?"

Jenni gestured at the elevators.

"I was on my way to my room," she said.

"Let me escort you to the elevator."

"That's very nice of you, but I'm okay now."

"I insist."

The guard grabbed Jenni's elbow and started toward the elevators. She lost her balance and started to topple to the floor. He caught her and put his arm around her waist. He started toward the elevator again and she had no choice but to hobble along with him. As they walked, his hand drifted from her waist to her ass. He gave her ass cheek a firm squeeze. Jenni jerked and almost fell again. And again, he saved her from falling on her ass.

When they got to the elevators, the guard pressed the up button and took his hand off her ass. Jenni was shaking as she crossed her arms under her breasts and stared at the floor. The guard leaned in close and spoke softly into her ear.

"Five bucks to feel your tits?" he said. "What a cheap bastard. Besides, I can tell they're real. Have a nice day."

The elevator arrived. Jenni waited for a middle-age couple to exit and then dashed inside. The guard smirked as he watched the elevator doors close. Jenni took a tiny step toward the wall panel to she could press the button for the twenty-third floor, slipped, and landed on her ass.

Chapter Four

Jenni rubbed her backside. She hadn't even seen her first client and already her ass was sore. As she watched the numbers climb toward twenty-three, she thought about what she was about to do. She was actually going to have sex with a stranger for money. It didn't matter whether she wanted to do it or not, it was going to happen.

She wondered what the man waiting for her looked like. That was something else that didn't matter. He could be the drunk in the Hawaiian shirt. If he was the man on the twenty-third floor who ordered her services, then she would take his money and let him do whatever he wanted to do to her.

She thought about the night before when Mr. Jones' four men had gangbanged her. They had broken her and left her wanting more. Images from that night flashed in mind. She could see their meaty cocks. Smell their musky scent. Taste their salty sperm. Her pussy twitched with the anticipation and desire that Johnny felt when he was on his way to card game. The rush he got from gambling was the rush she got from being fucked hard. A delicious shiver ran through her and her nipples grew erect.

That bastard Mr. Jones. He had saddled her with a new addiction.

The elevator reached the twenty-third floor and the doors slid open. The carpet absorbed the sound of Jenni's heels as she walked to the client's door. She knocked and waited. And then, she knocked again. And waited. Maybe she had the wrong room.

She was about to leave when a man opened the door. He narrowed his eyes at Jenni.

"Who are you?" he said.

"Jenni. You were expecting me."

He smacked his forehead.

"Right. Of course. Come on in."

The room was one of the moderately expensive suites, but not one of the overly extravagant suites that cost more than most folks' mortgage. The man had on a stripped dress shirt and a pair of chinos. He had rolled the sleeves of his shirt up to his elbows and was barefoot. He was tall and appeared to be in his forties. His dark brown hair was slicked back. Though he had a spare tire around his waist, he was a moderately handsome man.

He rushed over to the couch, but didn't sit down. He stood watching the wide screen TV. A basketball game was on.

"I'll be with you in just a minute," he said.

"You have to pay me first," Jenni said.

"What?"

"If you don't pay me, then I'll have to leave."

"Oh. Right. Sure."

He reached into his back pocket and took out his wallet. He took out five one hundred dollar bills and handed them to Jenni. She folded them up and put them in her pink wallet and put the wallet in her pink purse. She studied her clock.

"Your hour starts now," she said.

"I'll be with you as soon as the game is over. Help yourself to anything from the bar."

He pointed toward a wet bar in the corner of the room. A hallway led to a bedroom with a king bed. Jenni noticed that the man had an empty glass on the coffee table in front of him.

"Can I get you something?"

The man glanced at his glass and then back at the TV screen.

"Sure. Scotch on the rocks."

Jenni took the empty glass and went over to the bar. She got a fresh glass and dropped ice cubes into it. The cubes clinked on the glass. She picked out the bottle of Scotch. It was good stuff. She poured him a generous amount. Then, she poured herself a diet soda. She carried the drinks over to the couch. She put the man's drink on the table in front of him. She sat on the sofa and sipped her soda.

He sat next to her. He picked up the drink, took a sip, and nodded his approval.

"By the way," he said. "My name's Steve. I forgot your name."

"Jenni."

"Pleased to meet you, Jenni."

He ran his fingers through his oily hair. Jenni watched the game with him.

"Celtics and Knicks," she said. "Looks like it's a close game."

"I promise it's almost over."

"I can see that. Who did you bet on?"

Steve took another sip of this drink.

"I didn't bet on the game."

"Come on, Steve. You don't have a Boston or New York accent. The only reason why you'd be this wound up about the game was if you had some money riding on it."

The game was in the fourth quarter. The Celtics were winning but the score was close. Steve shrugged.

"Yeah. I bet on the game. I bet on the Knicks."

Jenni sipped her soda. She noticed her legs were too far apart. Not very ladylike and Steve could easily see up her skirt. She crossed her legs the way she'd seen women do it.

"What's the point spread?" she said.

"Celtics are the ten-point favorite," Steve said.

Jenni shook her head.

"I hope you didn't bet a lot of money," she said.

Steve turned to face her.

"What the fuck do you know?" he said.

"Women gamble same as men," Jenni said. "I've gambled on sports in the past and I know from experience that the odds are that you're going to lose this bet."

83

Steve swallowed the rest of his drink and went to the bar for a refill. He glared at Jenni. Jenni checked her watch. His hour was ticking away.

With less than a minute to go, the Celtics pulled ahead. The final seconds ticked down and the Celtics won by fourteen points. Steve clicked off the TV. He looked like someone had let the air out of him.

"Fuck me," he said.

"How much did you lose?" Jenni said.

"Five large."

"Ouch." Jenni looked at her watch. "Well, Steve. You still have fifteen minutes left. Maybe I can give you a quick hand job."

Steve waved his hand.

"No. Forget it. I couldn't get it up anyway. I'm too depressed. Keep the money."

"I wasn't planning on giving it back."

"Oh. Right. Sure. Just more money I lost in Vegas. What else is new?"

"Sorry, Steve." Jenni patted his leg. "I should probably go."

"Yeah. That's a good idea."

Jenni put her soda on the coffee table and stood. As she approached the door, she noticed that she was starting to get the hang of walking in heels. She was about to leave when she looked back at Steve. He was slumped on the couch, staring at the TV's blank screen. Jenni felt sorry for the poor bastard. Johnny had made hundreds of stupid bets before he learned how to work the system.

She went back to the couch, stood in front of Steve, and put her hand on her hip.

"Do you mind if I give you some friendly advice on how to bet on sports?" Jenni said.

Steve leaned forward. Jenni could tell he was staring at her tits. If he thought that was where she kept the secret to sports gambling, then he was a fucking idiot.

"Sure," Steve said. "That would be great."

She glanced at her watch. There wasn't time for sex, but there was time for advice.

"Which sports do you bet on?" she said.

"Just basketball," Steve said.

"How often?"

"Not very often."

"How do you decide which games to bet on?"

"I follow my instinct."

"How's that been working for you?"

Steve scratched his chin.

"Not too good."

Jenni put her purse on the coffee table and paced back and forth.

"Only bet on games that you have the best chance to win. The Celtics and the Knicks were too close in talent making it a toss-up. The percentages are better with mismatched games where you have a good idea of who is going to win. Don't bet big money on a whim. Bet the same amount on every game. You should win more games than you lose so at the end of the season you've made a profit."

Steve look gob smacked and then he grinned.

"You really do know your shit," he said. "Have you won a lot of money?"

"Yes," Jenni said.

She didn't tell him that she'd lost more than she won which was how she ended up in this hotel room with a pair of tits.

Steve jumped to his feet.

"That was great advice," Steve said. "And watching you school me on how to be a good gambler was so fucking sexy. I have a raging hard-on. Do I have time for a quickie?"

Jenni glanced at her watch.

"We have ten minutes."

"I only need five. Don't bother taking off your clothes. Just pull your panties down. I want to bend you over and take you from behind."

Jenni giggled. She couldn't believe she just giggled. She went around to other side of the couch. She wiggled her panties down to her ankles and slipped them over her shoe. She dipped a finger into her pussy to see if she needed to apply some lube, but she was slick and moist inside. Apparently, talking about gambling made her wet.

Steve unbuttoned his chinos and pulled them down with his underwear. He duck-walked over to Jenni with his bobbing erection leading the way. Jenni took a condom out of her purse, tore open the package with her teeth, took it out, and rolled it onto his cock. It was her first attempt to put a condom on a cock that wasn't hers and she got it on right away. It felt strangely natural.

She turned around and pulled her dress up, exposing her naked crotch. Steve moved in behind her. She felt his warm erection pressing against her ass. He leaned close to her so that she could smell the Scotch on his breath.

He fumbled as he attempted to get inside her. She reached between his legs and guided the mushroom head to her pussy lips.

"There," she said. "Put it in."

He thrust his hips and buried his cock into her wet pussy. Explosion went off inside Jenni. Finally, she had a cock inside her again. This was the fix she'd been craving. She bit her lower lip as Steve slid in and out of her.

Jenni held onto the back of the couch to keep from tipping over. Steve grabbed her hips and slammed into like a jackhammer. He grunted with each thrust. The smell of sex filled Jenni's nostrils, turning her on even more. She could feel his cock getting hotter and harder as he built toward his orgasm.

Then he stood still as he came inside her. His orgasm triggered her. She pressed her ass against his cock so that he was in deep inside as he could possibly go. She felt her pussy muscles clenched his hard cock as she milked the last of his sperm out of him.

Steve pulled out. Jenni sighed. She wanted more. She would have to wait until her next client.

"Damn!" Steve said.

Jenni held up her wrist and pointed at her watch.

"And we finished with two minutes to spare."

"Two minutes? Got any more gambling advice?"

Chapter Five

Logan leered at Jenni's French Fries.

"Are you going to eat those?" he said.

Jenni made a sour face.

"Everything tastes like sperm," she said.

Her last four clients had only wanted blow jobs. As a result, her jaw ached, her knees had rug burns, and she couldn't get the taste of sperm out of her mouth.

"Don't worry, honey," said the woman sitting next to her. "You get used to it."

The woman's name was Clarissa. Like Jenni and Lucy, she worked for Mr. Jones. Clarissa was African American. She was a big beautiful woman with big boobs, a big butt, and a big afro.

Clarissa had joined them after Jenni finished with her client at the MGM Grand. Logan had been driving the women to their appointments for hours when he announced it was time for a dinner break. He chose In-N-Out Burger.

"Does that mean you don't want your fries?" Logan said.

He reached for Jenni's fries and Clarissa smacked his hand.

"Get your own damn fries," she said. "Can't you see the girl's hungry?"

Logan had already devoured a Double-Double, fries, and a strawberry shake, but he announced that was still hungry.

"Look at that skinny ass," Clarissa said as she watched Logan head to the front counter to order more food. "I don't know where he puts it."

Jenni had ordered a hamburger, fries, and a diet soda. She had eaten half her hamburger and a few fries. Clarissa had finished her cheeseburger, fries, and large soda. She reached over and took a handful of Jenni's fries.

"Okay," Clarissa said. "Let's get this out of the way. I know you're Johnny. I'm Colin Harris."

Jenni's eyes widened.

"No fucking way. You're the highest ranked card player in the world. You're worth millions. I heard you had taken a hiatus from playing to spend some of that money and were living in Europe."

"Oh yeah," Clarissa said. "I've been all over Europe. I've been to Paris, Tuscany, Monte Carlo, the Riviera, and Caesars Palace without even having to get on an airplane. I just walk up and down the Las Vegas strip."

"I don't get it. You didn't have a losing streak. How did you end up in debt to Mr. Jones?"

Clarissa sucked on her straw but her cup was empty. She shook the cup and then set it aside.

"There are lots of ways to lose money in this town," she said. "For me, it was the ponies. I got addicted to horse racing and

lost everything. Including my dick. And I
really miss my dick."

Jenni glanced down at her crotch.

"I missed my dick too," she said.

Clarissa gave Jenni a sisterly hug.

"I was going to warn you," Clarissa
said.

Jenni narrowed her eyes at Clarissa.
"When?"

"I don't know. About a month ago. I
was at the casino to meet a client when I saw
you. You were talking to Mr. Jones. I couldn't
hear what you were talking about, but I can
tell when a player is begging to have his credit
extended. The word on the street was that you
were on a losing streak and were digging
yourself deeper and deeper into debt. I knew
it was just a matter of time before you ended
up in the basement getting a dose of nanobots
and a new pair of tits."

Jenni sank her fingers into Clarissa's
meaty thigh.

"If you knew what was going to happen, then why didn't you warn me?" she said.

Clarissa leaned back and gave Jenni a hard stare.

"Think about it," she said. "A hooker walks up to you and says buddy you're about to lose your dick. The best thing you can do right now is get the hell out of Vegas and never come back. Would you believe that hooker or would you call security?"

Jenni let go of Clarissa's thigh and clasped her hands together.

"You're right. I wouldn't have believed you." Jenni looked down at her breasts. "I'm still having trouble believing this is real."

Logan returned with a red tray. On the tray was his second strawberry shake and an order of animal style fries, fries covered in melted cheese, grilled onions, and Thousand Island Dressing. The women watched in disgust as he devoured his food.

"Hey, Logan," Clarissa said. "I told Jenni who I was. Why don't you come up for air long enough to tell her who you are?"

Jenni stared at Clarissa and then at Logan. He had a mouth full of fries. He wiped a smear of salad dressing off his face with a napkin and talked while he chewed.

"Laura McDonald," he said. "Maybe you've heard of me."

Jenni slapped the table top.

"The famous card cheat?" she said. "I thought you were dead and buried somewhere out in the fucking desert."

"As you can see," Clarissa said, gesturing at Logan. "The nanobots change men into women and women into men. How the hell this runt talked Mr. Jones into letting him join his team instead of peddling his cute ass on the street along is a mystery to me."

"That's right," Jenni said. "There's plenty of male prostitutes in town. How are you paying off your debt if you're not out there getting rug burns on your knees along with the rest of us?"

Logan shrugged and stuffed more gooey fries into his mouth.

"I wouldn't have cared if they had made me sell my ass," Logan said. "I'd sucked plenty of dicks and been fucked in the butt as a woman. I told them they'd done me a favor by turning me into a man and I would show my gratitude by taking any job they gave me. Mr. Jones figured I was more valuable as an errand boy than as a gigolo."

Clarissa snatched one of Logan's fries and popped in into mouth. Logan grinned as she sucked the cheese off her finger.

"You don't miss being a woman?" Clarissa said.

"Fuck no," Logan said. "The clitoris is a wonderful thing. I suggest you ladies spend some quality time getting intimate with your clits. It can deliver earthshaking orgasms that no male orgasm can compete with. But it's an elusive bitch that has a way of disappearing and reappearing and sometimes it likes to be attached and other times it's so tender you can't touch it. But as for the cock. It's always ready to go. Which means I don't have to get in the mood for sex. I'm always in the mood. And see this food here. When I was a woman, this shit would have gone straight to my hips and it would take me years to get rid of it. As a man, I'll hit the gym tomorrow and burn most of it off by before lunchtime."

Logan scooped a handful of fries into his mouth and washed them down by slurping on his strawberry shake. Clarissa rolled her eyes and then leaned in close to Jenni.

"Logan's an asshole," she said. But what he said about the clitoris is true."

Chapter Six

Logan parked the town car in the parking lot of Circus Circus. The gaudy neon clown sign for the hotel and casino beckoned Jenni to go inside. It was after midnight so the free circus acts were done for today. The acrobats were no longer airborne and the clowns were either asleep or beeping each other's horn.

On their way here, Logan had dropped off Clarissa at Caesars Palace and would pick her up when she was done. He swiveled around in the front seat to look back at Jenni.

"This is probably your last client of the night," Logan said. "He booked you for two hours."

"Really?" Jenni said.

Most clients booked an hour and were done in fifteen minutes. This client's expectations seemed overly optimistic.

"He specifically requested you," Logan said.

Jenni felt a chill run down her spine.

"You didn't tell people who I was, did you?" she said.

Logan held up his hand.

"Calm down," he said. "Mr. Jones would never do that. If word got out that he'd turned male derelict gamblers into female hookers, it would be more trouble for him than for you ladies."

"Then how does this guy know who I am?"

"Only a small circle of Mr. Jones' employees knows about the nanobots. They know because like me they're directly involved with the program. This guy is one of them."

"I thought I was off limits to you guys."

"Not at all. We can't fuck you for free. But we can pay for it just like any other client and this guy is paying full price."

Jenni gnawed on her knuckle.

"Who is it?" she said.

"I can't tell you that," Logan said. "He wants it to be a surprise."

Jenni had a bad feeling about this, but she had no choice. Until she paid off her debt to Mr. Jones, this was her life. She got out of the car.

It felt odd entering a hotel that catered to families so she could have sex with a stranger for money. She supposed she wasn't the first hooker to meet a John in this place. Plenty of fathers probably had a whore come to their room to relieve the pressure of family obligations while wives and kids were out spending their money at the circus.

Despite the late hour, the lobby was buzzing with activity. As Jenni strode toward the elevators, she passed way too many kids up past their bedtimes. She'd slowly gotten used to walking in heels and was no longer worried about falling on her ass. She'd noticed that she'd begun to swing her hips and from the way men were staring at her ass, she imagined that they had noticed too.

Her client's room was on the top floor of the West Tower. As she rode the elevator, she wondered who was up there waiting for her. She couldn't imagine it would be Peter. She got the impression that he didn't like her. Even when he was shoving his cock inside her, he didn't seem to like her.

She hoped it wasn't Bruno. She didn't care that he was so hairy, especially on his back. She'd begun to notice men's body odor and his was atrocious. She'd have to hold her nose while he grunted on top of her.

Her stomach did a flip at the thought that it might be Mr. Jones. She wouldn't be able to handle that. Besides, if he wanted to fuck her, he would probably do it in his office so he could watch the casino floor at the same time.

It could be Keith.

Her stomach did another flip, but for different reasons. She missed his enormous black cock and she hated herself for missing it. When he had held her down and plowed into her so deeply that she thought he'd rearrange her internal organs, he had broken her into pieces and put her back together as a whore addicted to cock. She could feel the moisture growing between her legs as she remembered every detail of his veiny cock. She could almost smell its earthy aroma. She licked her lips with the desire to taste him again and feel the heaviness of his balls in her mouth. She reached up and touched her erect nipples. Her cheeks flushed with anticipation. Could it really be Keith? Did he miss her pussy as much as she missed his cock?

The elevator dinged. She looked up. It wasn't her floor. She pulled her hands down to her side as a couple boarded the elevator. They saw that they top floor button had been pushed, glanced at Jenni, and the stared at the doors. Jenni worried the handle on her pink purse as they rode in silence. When they reached the top floor, the couple headed to the left and Jenni went right.

103

Her client's room was at the end of a hallway. As she approached it, she could hear techno dance music playing very loudly from someone's room. When she reached the door, she realized it was coming from her client's room. She banged on the door. She expected to have to bang on the door many times to be heard over the music, but the door opened immediately.

The man holding the door open wore black jeans and a black cowboy hat, and nothing else. He was bare-chested and barefoot. Jenni stared at him in disbelief.

"Oh my God," she said. "Not you."

"Hello, Johnny," he said. "Come on in. I've been waiting for you."

Chapter Seven

The name of the man at the door was Viktor Orlov. He was born in Russia and had been a member of the Russian Mafia. Jenni had no idea why Viktor immigrated to America or how he ended up in Las Vegas and quite frankly had no interest in finding out.

"Don't stand out there in cold," Viktor said. "Come in. Come in."

Jenni resisted the urge to turn and run and entered the hotel room. She never liked Viktor. He was a major league asshole, but he was also Mr. Jones' bodyguard. Now that she thought about it, Jenni was surprised that Viktor wasn't one of the guys who gangbanged her in the casino's basement yesterday. Maybe he had a dentist appointment and had to miss the fun.

Viktor sauntered over to a table where he had lined up an ice bucket, glasses, club soda, and a bottle of Chivas Regal.

"May I get you drink, Johnny?" he said.

"It's Jenni now," she said. "And yes. Give me a drink."

Jenni had avoided any offers of alcohol from her earlier clients, but she was going to need a good stiff drink before she had sex with this douchebag. Viktor dropped ice cubes into two glasses, filled the glass with the expensive Scotch and added a dash of club soda. He handed Jenni one of the glasses. He held his glass up to clink glasses with her, but she ignored him and took a generous sip from her drink. It burned her throat and spread a pleasant warmth in her stomach.

"I heard from the boys that out of all the men who've undergone Mr. Jones' special treatment, none of them have come out as gorgeous as Johnny," Viktor said as he walked around Jenni. "I had to see for myself and they were right. I never would have imagined that you Johnny would have such nice titties. And what a great ass."

He lightly smacked her butt. Jenni gritted her teeth.

"Call me Jenni. It's the name Mr. Jones gave me and I'm sure he would prefer you call me that until I can reclaim my real name."

"Yes. Yes. Of course." Viktor began dancing to the techno music. "Come. Dance with me, Jenni."

Jenni held out her palm.

"You know the rules," she said. "Pay me first and then I'll do whatever you want me to do."

The gamblers' nickname for Viktor was Rent. He was so easy to beat in a poker game, that they joked that they only played cards with him when you needed rent money. The joke was actually true. The gamblers wouldn't let him join their games unless they needed cash because Viktor was such a boring blowhard.

During card games, he yammered on and on about how amazing he was in bed. He claimed he could fuck for hours and that after sex with him, women worshipped him and begged him for more. But then right after he bragged about how great he was in bed, he would turn around and tell an embarrassing story like how a hooker once made him squirt the second she put his cock in her mouth by sticking her thumb up his ass.

"You've taken to being a whore really well," Viktor said. "You know to ask for money first."

He dug into his jean pocket and pulled out a roll of money which he handed to Jenni. She counted the bills. It was enough for two hours of her time. She put the roll in her purse.

"Okay," she said. "I'm not much of a dancer, but if that's what you want me to do then I'll dance."

Jenni shuffled her feet from side to side and swung her arms. Johnny had been a lousy dancer and becoming a woman hadn't magically changed Jenni into a dancing queen.

Viktor didn't seem to care. He was too busy staring at the way her tits jiggled when she moved.

"Every new girl given three rules, right?" Viktor said. "Rule one. Money before sex. You got money and soon we have sex." He danced around behind her and rubbed his crotch against her ass. "Rule two. No free sex. Silly rule since rule one already covers that." He wrapped his arm around her waist and pressed against her back while continuing to dance with her. "Rule three. No gambling. Tell me, Johnny. I mean, Jenni. Tell me what happens to bad girls who break rule number three?"

Jenni felt an icy chill run down her spine. She tried to break away, but he was too strong.

"A bullet in the head," she stammered.

Viktor put the side of his face against hers. He sniffed her hair.

"That's right," he said. "Bullet in head." He pointed his finger at the other side of her head. "And you know who Mr. Jones calls when a bad girl breaks rule number three?"

"You?"

"That's right. Break rule number three and I will come for you. Nobody where you go. No matter where you hide. I will find you and ... Boom!"

Jenni yelped and Viktor laughed.

"Listen, Rent," Jenni said. "I swear you won't have to worry about me breaking any rules."

Viktor turned her around and slapped her face. Jenni fell to her knees. Her face stung where he'd struck her.

"Don't ever call me that name!" Viktor roared. "You think I don't know what you pigs say about me behind my back? But now, I get my revenge. Go in bedroom and take off your fucking clothes, you filthy whore."

Jenni got to her feet.

"Is it okay if I go to the bathroom first?" she said. "I really have to pee."

"Yeah, sure. The bathroom is right over there."

Jenni dashed into the bathroom and locked the door. She pulled down her panties, sat on the toilet, and emptied her bladder. Her hands were shaking. She didn't want to be in this hotel room for another second. Certainly, she was allowed to refuse to service a client. Especially, if she was afraid that the client was going to cause her bodily harm.

She looked at her face in the mirror. Her cheek was pink from where Viktor had slapped her. She knew she couldn't leave. Viktor was close to Mr. Jones and until her debt was paid, she belonged to Mr. Jones.

Her knees felt weak as she came out of the bathroom. The room was quiet. Viktor had turned off the techno dance music. She didn't see him and for a brief moment she thought maybe he was gone and she could leave. But then, she knew where he was. He was waiting for her in the bedroom.

Viktor was sprawled out on the king bed. He'd gotten rid of the cowboy hat, but still had on his jeans. He looked at her with hungry eyes.

"Let's see what you've got," he said.

With fumbling hands, Jenni took off her clothes. Goosebumps rose on her skin as she exposed it for the Russian hitman. When she removed her bra, and let her breasts fall out, Viktor gave a wolf whistle.

"Look at those titties!" he said. "They are fucking magnificent."

Jenni blushed.

She slipped off her shoes before taking off her panties. She stood naked at the foot of the bed and waited his instructions. He scooted over to her. He sat on the edge of the bed and nuzzled his head between her breasts. He grabbed a tit and sucked on the nipple. Despite herself, the nipple grew erect and she felt tingling through her body.

"Take off my pants," he said.

Jenni unbuttoned his jeans, pulled down the zipper, and worked the jeans down to his ankles. He didn't have on underwear. As she tossed his pants aside, she wasn't surprised to see that he had shaved his pubic hair or that he was wearing a cock ring. That would explain why he was able to fuck for a long time.

Despite the fact that Viktor scared the beejezus out of Jenni, she had to admit that he had a nice-looking cock. It wasn't as big as Keith's, but it was thick and had to be at least nine inches. She stroked it gently. Viktor leaned back his head and moaned.

"That feels good," he said. "But your mouth would feel better."

Jenni could take a hint. She kneeled between his legs and held his warm cock in her hand. She licked the head while fondling his balls. Then she stuck his cock into her mouth and sucked on it.

Viktor grabbed her hair and forced his shaft down her throat. She gasped and choked but managed to keep sucking. She wished she could do what that other hooker did, stick her thumb up his ass so that he could come right away. But she wasn't sure it would work since he had the cock ring on.

After just a few thrusts, Viktor let go of Jenni's head. She pulled away, gasping for air. Drool hung off her chin. She started to stroke his saliva coated cock, but he slipped away from her and went to the other side of the bed.

Viktor snatched a small glass bottle off the bedside table and twisted off the cap. He held the open bottle under his nose and inhaled.

Just as Jenni wasn't surprised to see Viktor wearing a cock ring, she wasn't surprised to see him sniffing Amyl nitrite, better known as poppers. He was using every trick he could come up with to maintain an erection.

"Did you take Viagra tonight?" Jenni said.

"No," Johnny said indignantly. "I prefer Cialis."

Jenni was actually glad to hear that Johnny had taken a boner pill. After an evening of blow jobs, her pussy was itching for a meat injection. She was disappointed that it wasn't going to be Keith's massive black cock plowing her, but she would take what she could get. Even if it was a douchebag like Viktor.

"Come," Viktor said, patting the mattress. "Get on all fours."

Jenni climbed onto the bed and go on her hands and knees. She faced the window so she couldn't see Viktor behind her. She heard a squirting sound. She looked over her shoulder. Viktor was squeezing lube into the palm of his hand. He slathered it onto his erection. He squeezed more lube into his hand and turned toward her. She expected to feel the cool goo on her pussy, but instead he rubbed it around her butthole.

"Um, Viktor," she said nervously. "Just so I can prepare mentally, please tell me what you're about to do."

"Have you not done anal yet?"

"No. I haven't"

Viktor worked the lube inside her ass, first with one finger and then with two.

"This is too fucking good. I get to pop your ass cherry."

"Yeah. About that. Are you sure you wouldn't prefer to fuck my pussy instead? It's still very tight."

"No pussy is tight as butthole. You're a lucky bitch. I'm very good at anal. When I'm done you're going to beg me to fuck you in the ass every fucking day."

Viktor hiked onto the bed and got behind Jenni. She could feel his hard cock pressing against her ass cheeks.

"Arch your back," he said. "Spread legs a little wider."

Jenni did as he instructed. Her ass was more exposed. She trembled in anticipation. She felt his cock nudged against her ass. He eased it into her. Incredible pain wracked her body. She thought she would faint from the agony. She bit her lip to keep from begging him to take it out.

He eased in another inch. The pain increased. Her arms shook and sweat formed on her upper lip. He eased out and she felt immense relief, but then he pushed back in.

Only this time, it didn't hurt as bad. Her anus began to relax and open up. His cock began to create pleasant sensations inside her. With each thrust, she felt more shivers of pleasure.

Viktor smacked her ass and Jenni squeaked.

"You like that?" he said.

He smacked her again. Jenni giggled. It didn't hurt. It added to the dirty pleasure. Jenni pulled a pillow over and laid her head

117

on it. This lifted her ass even higher. Viktor grabbed her hips and humped her steadily.

Jenni couldn't believe it. She was enjoying getting fucked by Viktor. With his attention focused on lasting as long as humanly possible, Jenni reached between her legs and played with her pussy. It was slick with her juices. Jenni got into a rhythm and rubbed her pussy in unison with Viktor humping her ass.

Her breasts swayed with each thrust. The pressure built up inside her. She forgot about the pain when he first entered her asshole as his cock and her fingers drove her toward a cliff of ecstasy.

"All those times you take my money and laugh behind my back," Viktor said. "Now who is laughing? Now I fuck you after all the times you fucked me."

"Oh yeah, baby," Jenni moaned. "Fuck me. Fuck me so fucking hard."

Her thighs shook as shudders rippled through her. She felt a growing sensation in her pussy that spread all through her body. She rubbed her clitoris faster and faster. Her sensitive nipples brushed against the sheets.

Viktor ground down even harder and Jenni couldn't hold back any longer. Waves of pleasure exploded inside her. Fluid gushed out of her pussy and ran down her thighs. Her moans were muffled by the pillow.

Viktor didn't slow down. He kept plowing into Jenni. She kept rubbing her pussy and her second orgasm erupted inside her.

Her knees buckled during the third orgasm and she slid to her stomach. Still, Viktor kept fucking her ass.

She grabbed handfuls of the bedsheets as her fourth orgasm rippled through her. She never took her hand away from her clitoris while Viktor showed extraordinary stamina.

Her pussy was sore, but she still masturbated herself to a fourth mind-numbing orgasm even though Viktor was noticeably slowing down.

Jenni finally had enough orgasms and just relaxed as Viktor continued to slam his cock into her ass. Her fingers and thighs were slick with her pussy juices. She was beyond pain or pleasure as her ass cheeks bounced with each thrust. Finally, Viktor let out a strangled cry and Jenni felt the swell of his cock as he exploded inside her ass. When he was done coming, he collapsed on top of her.

Breathing hard and sweating heavily, Viktor pulled his limp cock out of her ass and rolled off of her. She wrapped her arms around the pillow and felt his sperm dripping between her ass cheeks.

"I have dominated you," Viktor said. "From now on, every man you sleep with will pale in comparison to me. You will dream of me. Your ass will pucker at the thought of my cock. If you see me, you will make a fool of yourself by begging me to fuck you again. But I won't. I will make you suffer. And then, maybe if I'm in a good mood I will give you the pleasure of my magnificent cock again."

Jenni buried her head in the pillow to keep Viktor from hearing her laugh. He was as much a boring blowhard during sex as he was when he was playing cards. Though he did teach her that anal could be enjoyable, he didn't dominate her. She was more responsible for her orgasms tonight than he was.

If it made him happy to think that her ass would pucker at the thought of his cock, then that was fine with her. Her job was to make her clients happy. Jenni checked her watch. Viktor had managed to last twenty minutes. Pretty good, but nowhere near two hours. She wondered how quickly he would have come if he hadn't been wearing the cock ring or taken Viagra.

Chapter Eight

The first hint of sunrise was on the horizon when Logan dropped Jenni off at the motel. She was exhausted and this was just her first day on the job. Her feet ached, her bra straps were biting into her shoulders, she had a nasty taste in her mouth, and she had to take small steps because her ass was sore from Viktor's anal assault.

She unlocked the door to room thirteen and stepped inside. The lights were on. She couldn't remember if she had left them on or not. But then she saw why they were on. Peter was seated at the table. He wore a sport coat, slacks, and a dress shirt. His legs were crossed and he had an annoying smirk on his face.

"Rough night?" he said.

Jenni shrugged. She sat her tender butt gingerly on the bed across from him. She snapped open her pink purse and took out a large roll of bills.

"I was wondering how and when we would do this," she said as she handed the roll over to Peter.

He took the roll and straightened out the pile of bills.

"Depends," he said. "Since this was your first time, I'd come to you. We'll work out a method."

He counted the money quickly and chuckled.

"We keep track of your jobs so we know how much you're supposed to give us at the end of the night," he said. "There have been way too many times when a girl has shorted me, but you're the first girl to overpay me."

Jenni crossed her arms under her breasts.

"You didn't know about Lucy," she said. "She was my first client today."

Peter leaned back and laughed.

"Did she pay you three hundred to go down on you?" he said.

Jenni's brow knitted in confusion. "Yes. She did."

"You're not the first girl she pulled that trick on. That three hundred is from Mr. Jones. It's your walking around money. She was supposed to give it to you and explain what it was for."

Peter counted out three hundred in twenties and handed them to Jenni. She folded them in half and put them in her purse. Peter got ready to leave.

"Wait," Jenni said. "Can I ask you a question?"

Peter sat back down.

"Sure," he said. "You can ask me anything you want."

"Would you consider this a typical night?"

"For you?"

"Yeah. For me. Is this a typical number of clients? Is this the amount of money I should be making every night?"

Peter grinned.

"It varies, of course, but yes, this was a fairly typical night. You can expect to see the same number of clients and earn the same amount of money."

"I'm pretty good at math. At this rate, it's going to take me at least a year to pay off Mr. Jones. Maybe even two years."

"It could even take you three or four years." Peter snorted. "You just now figuring this out? Did you really think it would be that easy to get your cock back?"

Jenni felt tears welling up in her eyes. She didn't know if her emotions were so raw and near the surface because of the bizarre situation she was in or if it was because of being a woman.

"I don't think I can handle four years in this body," she said. "I'm afraid if I spent that much time like this, I'll lose my identity as Johnny. Especially after you got me addicted to cock. I'm afraid if I don't get my cock back soon I'll end up staying like this forever."

Peter stood and stuffed the money Jenni made that evening into his pants pocket. He sneered down at Jenni.

"I have to go," he said. "I can't stand watching women cry."

The tears flowed down Jenni's face, ruining her make-up.

"Mr. Jones can't do this to me. This must be some other way I can pay him back."

"Damn it, Johnny. You got yourself into this mess. Now you have to live with it."

Peter left the room. Jenni sobbed and then dragged herself into the bathroom. She washed her face and stared at her reflection in the mirror.

She gritted her teeth. She'd find a way to pay off Mr. Jones sooner. Johnny knew how to hustle for money. That meant she could figure out a way to hustle money. Johnny only had his wits, his charm, and his ability to bluff his way through any situation. She had all that and a body desired by men and women. She would use her body to earn more money than she was making now. She would pay her debt, get her cock back, and be Johnny again. And it wasn't going to take her four years to do it. If she played her cards right, she might even be able to do it in four months. She just had to be Jenni a little while longer.

The End

GENDER SWAP
GAMBLER 3

Chapter One

Jenni stood at the edge of the pool and watched the first rays of the morning sun glint off the smooth surface of the water. She tucked her hair into her swim cap, and then dived in. The bracing cold water cleared the cobwebs out of her head. She sliced through the water as she swam her morning laps.

A month had gone by since Mr. Jones had turned Johnny into Jenni. Or more accurately, a month had gone by since Mr. Jones had turned Johnny into a call girl named Jenni Jones who sold her body every night to earn back the massive amount of money she owed the casino.

It had been a difficult month to say the least.

She'd had to adjust from being a swaggering alpha male to being a subservient female sex worker. As if her life wasn't fucked up enough, Mr. Jones had gotten her hooked on cock.

Jenni was obsessed with cocks, their girth, their funky smell, the network of veins, the way they grew in size and stiffness, the drop of pre-come that formed in the slit. the way a man moaned when she put his cock in her mouth, the way some cocks grew so hot before the man ejaculated that she thought he would scorch her insides. She loved the salty taste of sperm. Every time a client pulled his cock out, she got moist between her legs. Her pussy's Pavlovian response to cock was a constant source of humiliation to the part of her that was still Johnny.

Jenni spent her days sleeping on the bed of her motel room and her nights working on the beds of her clients' hotel rooms. When she returned at her room in the early morning hours, she had trouble falling asleep even though she was physically exhausted. As Johnny, she'd had the same problem. After an all-night poker game, he would be wound up to go straight to bed. To unwind, he would change into his running clothes and jog for an hour.

Jenni tried that and quickly decided it was a bad idea for many reasons. Even though she wore an athletic bra that held her big tits in a viselike grip, they still bounced around and she ended up with sore tits. The motel was in a rundown neighborhood with lots of boarded up buildings. Only a few car repair shops and warehouses were still open. Johnny wouldn't have thought twice about walking through the area, but as a woman, she felt that she was in constant danger.

Men stopped what they were doing to watch her jog by. Many of them shouted out the things they would like to do to her sexually. Men in cars drove next to her and asked her if she'd like to go for a ride. Her survival instinct trumped her addiction to cock and she ran as quickly as she could back to the motel. That was when she decided to swim laps instead.

Jenni quickly discovered that she enjoyed swimming at dawn. Her one-piece swimsuit held her breasts snugly and the crotch didn't ride up her ass until she got out of the pool. She always had the pool to herself. Once in the water, the rest of the world was shut out. She didn't hear the constant traffic of the Las Vegas freeway or the constant construction of the city. In the pool, all she could hear was her own breathing and the splash of the water made by her limbs.

She found she did her best thinking while doing her laps. And what she thought about most was how to pay off her debt quicker than how she was paying it off now. At the rate she was making money now she would be stuck as a woman for at least three more years. She had to find a way to earn more. If only she were allowed to gamble. If Mr. Jones would let her play poker, she could make the money she owed the casino in less than a month. Then again, it was playing poker that got her into this mess. She'd have to find another way.

Swimming in the pool wasn't the only time she was alone. Jenni rarely saw anyone at the motel. She was certain that she wasn't the only debt-ridden gambler turned into a call girl with a nanobot injection living at the motel. She knew of at least two others, Lucy and Clarissa. Jenni occasionally saw Lucy lugging a big blue IKEA bag full of clothes, but she never saw Clarissa.

Jenni didn't notice the absence of other people at first. Adjusting to her new reality consumed all her energy during those first days. She didn't even know the name of the motel. She just knew that she stayed in room thirteen until Logan came to get her at night.

Eventually, Jenni ventured out of her room during the day. The casino had no one around to make sure she didn't try to get away. They didn't need to. If she left before paying her debt, then she'd never get her cock back. She'd never be Johnny again and would be forced to stay Jenni Jones forever.

It wasn't until she saw the motel's sign that she realized that she didn't even know the place was called the Moonbeam Motor Lodge. The No Vacancy neon sign was on even though there were only three cars in the parking lot. She went into the front office and met the manager, Monique.

It seemed that Monique's main job was to sit at the desk in case someone ignored the no vacancy sign. That only happened once in a blue moon, so Monique was thrilled to have company. Jenni didn't have to prod her for information. Monique poured them both a cup of tea and talked non-stop for an hour.

During that hour, Jenni figured out that Monique was not a victim of Mr. Jones' nanobots. She was in her late fifties. Judging from the stories she told about her younger days, she was a hell raiding party girl before she settled down and got married.

For twenty-five years, Monique and her husband, Carl, owned and operated the Moonbeam Motor Lodge. Business had been steady until the latest slump in the economy and the neighborhood turned to shit. If that weren't bad enough, Carl got the cancer and died.

Monique put the place up for sale. Nobody was interested. But then Mr. Jones came to see her. The casino wanted to buy the motel on the condition that Monique continue on as manager. Monique didn't think she could run the motel on her own, but Mr. Jones assured her that her job would be easy. Only special guests of the casino would be staying on an extended basis. And the casino would take care of the day to day operation. Monique just had to sit at the front desk. If Monique knew anything about the motel's special guests, she didn't share that information with Jenni.

Jenni finished her laps and climbed out of the pool. She took off her swim cap

135

and rung out her hair before wrapping it with a towel. Lucy had taught her how to wrap a towel into a turban. She used another towel to dry her arms and legs and then wrapped it around her waist. She slipped on a pair of sandals and picked up her room key.

When she turned the corner of her building, she was surprised to see a housekeeping cart parked outside her room. Maybe she was finally going to meet someone else associated with the Moonbeam Motor Lodge.

Chapter Two

Every morning Jenni returned to her room after work, she always found that her room had been cleaned while she was out. Jenni lived such a Spartan life that her room never needed much cleaning.

The clean room surprised her for two reasons. First, that the casino bothered to provide maid service for their call girls, and second, that they had the maids clean at night while the escorts were out. Jenni never saw the maids.

But here was a housekeeping cart outside her room in the morning. Jenni poked her head inside the door and saw a man making her bed. He wore a T-shirt, plaid pajama pants, and Crocs. Jenni entered the room and stood behind him.

"Hey, mister," Jenni said. "Hope I'm not interrupting you." The man turned to face Jenni and she saw that it wasn't a man. It was a woman. Jenni blushed. "I'm sorry. I didn't

137

mean to call you mister. You had your back to me and you have short hair."

The maid placed her hands on her hips.

"It's okay," she said. "I'm an ugly broad so I can understand the mistake."

Jenni was going to argue, but the woman was right. She was unattractive. She had a flat nose, beady eyes, and a pointed chin. She had pancake breasts and narrow hips. It didn't help that she wore no make-up and didn't comb her hair.

"Normally, I don't clean rooms this early," the maid said, "but I noticed that you swim in the morning and I was hoping to get yours out of the way. See, I got plans tonight and I don't want to be late."

Jenni narrowed her eyes at the woman. There was something about her face and her accent that seemed very familiar. She snapped her fingers.

"Brian!" Jenni said. "Brian Summers! It's me, Johnny."

The woman shrugged her shoulders.

"Yeah, I knew it was you, Johnny," she said. "But I'm not Brian any more than you're Johnny. It's Brittany. Brittany Jones."

"Brittany?"

"Mr. Jones has got a real sense of humor when it comes to naming us broads doesn't he?"

"Yeah. He named me Jenni Jones."

"Jenni's better than fucking Brittany."

"Whatever. Bring it over here and give me a hug."

Brittany and Jenni hugged. Gamblers were by nature cutthroat competitors. Close friendships were rare. However, that didn't prevent some gamblers from becoming friends. Though they went months without seeing or talking to each other, Brian was Johnny's best friend.

Brittany suggested they go to her room. Jenni followed as Brittany wheeled her cart to an adjacent building. She left the cart in the walkway and unlocked the door to room thirty-nine.

Jenni whistled in amazement. It wasn't just a room. It was a full apartment and it was huge. If someone took Jenni's room and multiplied it by three, they would easily fit inside Brittany's apartment. She had a full bathroom, a living room, and a large bedroom. There was even kitchenette.

Brittany may have cleaned the other rooms, but her place was a pig sty. Styrofoam clamshells filled with scraps of decaying fast food were piled on the dining table next to empty beer bottles. An overflowing ashtray was on the coffee table.

"Want a beer?" Brittany said as she opened the frig.

"Sure," Jenni said. "I'm off duty."

Brittany handed Jenni a beer. She took a sip. It was her first taste of alcohol since the transformation. The two women settled in the living room. Brittany turned on the widescreen TV and flipped the channels until she found a poker game. Jenni's room didn't have a TV. Brittany took a swig of her beer and glared at the screen.

"You got to hand it to Mr. Jones," Brittany said. "He really knows how to hurt a guy. He could've just broken my legs, but instead he turned me into my mother."

Jenni felt something digging into her butt. She checked the chair she was sitting in and found a soda can jammed between the cushions.

"That's funny," Jenni said. "Turned you into your mother."

"I'm not joking," Brittany said. "I look just like my fucking mother. She was an ugly broad too." Brittany gave Jenni the once over. "I see your mom was a real looker."

Jenni shrugged.

"I wouldn't know," she said. "I was adopted. I have no idea what my mother looked like."

"Well now you do. Just look in the fucking mirror. Don't you get it? The nanobots changed our gender. They turned us into what we would have been if we'd been born with two X chromosomes instead of an X and a Y."

Jenni let this sink in.

"We just got to get our Y back," she said.

"I heard that," Brittany said.

She and Jenni clinked their beer bottles.

Brittany went into the kitchenette and searched the cabinets until she found an unopened bag of pork rinds. She tore it open and shared it with Jenni. They watched the poker game in silence. Jenni was torn between wanting to get out of her wet bathing suit and hanging out with her old friend. She felt clammy and sleepy, so she knew she'd have to leave soon.

"How long have you been...," Jenni said. "You know."

"Walking around with a pussy?" Brittany said. "Two years. I still have to serve three more years in this body, this prison, until I'm free."

"Five years?"

Brittany drained her bottle of beer and belched.

"They tried to have me pay off my debt the way they got you doing it. You know. The old fashion way. On my back. But it didn't take. I give Mr. Jones credit for trying. They had me dress up in slutty clothes, did my hair and make-up, the whole nine yards. But you know what they say. You can put lipstick on a pig, but it's still a pig."

Jenni could hear the bitterness in Brittany's voice. She may not have wanted to be turned into a woman, but rejection hurt no matter what the circumstances. Jenni felt a pang of guilt. Johnny had kicked a few escorts out of his room for being less beautiful than a swimsuit model.

"When I show up for a job," Jenni said, "the guy doesn't seem to care what I look like as long as I get on my knees and suck his dick."

"They care," Brittany said. "Believe me they care. When I showed up, they kicked me out. Every fucking time. So, Mr. Jones decides that I have to work off my debt a different way. And that's how I ended up as a maid."

Jenni stood to go to the bathroom and the room spun. The beer combined with the need for sleep caught up with her.

"I have to go, Brittany," she said. "I'm dead on my feet. But I'll come by to see you soon."

"Come over tonight," Brittany said.

"I can't. I have to work."

"Not tonight. Mr. Jones gives us one night off a month."

"I have the night off? Why didn't anybody tell me?"

Brittany laughed.

"Don't get your panties in a wad. I'm telling you now. Come back here around seven. Everybody will be here. We drink beer, play cards, and shoot the shit. Just like the old days."

Jenni grinned.

"I'd like that. See you tonight."

Chapter Three

At 7:00PM, Jenni knocked on Brittany's door. Brittany answered. She wore a burgundy velour tracksuit and tennis shoes. She wore a little bit of make-up and had even combed her hair. She gave Jenni a bro hug and ushered her into the apartment.

Jenni was shocked. When she had come by early this morning, the place was a mess, but now it was spotless. It even smelled nice. In the kitchenette was a tray of deli sandwiches, boxes of pizza, and bags of chips. There were bottles of Vodka, Bourbon, and Tequila next to glasses, and mixers.

"Do you still drink Bourbon?" Brittany said, "Or do you just drink white wine now?"

Jenni grabbed her breasts. "These didn't change my preference for alcohol."

Brittany chuckled as she prepared a Bourbon and soda. She handed Jenni the drink and then led her into the living room.

Four women were playing poker at a table in the middle of the room. Jenni recognized Lucy and Clarissa, but not the other two women. They all wore velour tracksuits except for one woman who wore a cotton night gown. She was also the only woman other than Brittany wearing make-up. Jenni wore yoga pants, a Las Vegas tourist T-shirt, and sandals.

Brittany put her arm around Jenni's shoulder.

"Jenni," Brittany said. "Let me introduce you to your sisters. I understand you've already met Lucy and Clarissa so I'll skip them." She pointed at each woman as she introduced them. "This lovely Greek woman with the exotic features and amazing full figure body is Nadia and that slim and stacked beauty with Barbra Streisand's face is Sheila. Ladies, this is sister, Jenni Jones."

Nadia shook hands with Jenni. She wore multiple bracelets and her long nails were painted bright pink.

"Pull up a chair, Jenni," Nadia said. "We'll deal you in on the next hand."

"I thought you'd never ask," Jenni said.

Jenni dragged a chair over and the women scooted over to make room for her. Her fingers ached to hold cards again. Instead of money, the women were betting Tic Tacs. Jenni smiled. Every night Logan picked Jenni up for work, he gave her a container of Tic Tacs. Jenni figured it was to make sure she didn't have dick breath. Jenni noticed that sitting in the corner of the room was a stack of boxes filled with Tic Tac containers.

"I get it," Jenni said. "We're not allowed to gamble with money, but the casino doesn't care if we gamble with breath mints."

A few hands later, she was on the verge of tears because she was so happy to be playing poker again. It didn't matter that they were playing with breath mints instead of money. Gambling was in her blood.

Every gambler has his or her own style. The way they hold their cards. The way they place their bets. The way they watch the other players. Jenni could tell from the women played who they had been before Mr. Jones gave them a dose of nanobots. She already knew that Brittany was Brian Summers, Lucy was Luke Lee, and Clarissa was Colin Harris, all big money winners on the poker circuit until they started losing.

But now she knew that Nadia was Nick Cosmos, one of the finest chard sharks to ever play the game and Sheila was Stu Rothstein, one of the toughest players Johnny had ever faced.

The door flew open and a Mexican woman in a maid's outfit waddled in. She was short, tubby, and not so much ugly as extremely plain. She grabbed a beer out of the frig and pulled up a chair.

"Where you been, Eva?" Brittany said.

"One of the maids called in sick and I had to fill in," Eva said. "Got here as soon as I could. As you can see, I didn't even bother to change."

Once Eva was dealt into the game, she took a cigar out of her purse and lit it up. Jenni grinned. She had been fairly certain that Eva was Ernesto Flores, but the cigar gave it away. Ernesto was known for his stinky cigars.

Jenni did well against these excellent players and soon had a respectable pile of Tic Tacs in front of her.

"How are you adjusting?" Sheila said.

Jenni knew she was asking her how she was dealing with being a woman.

"There are times when I still feel like I'm in somebody else's body," she said.

"You get used to it."

"But I don't want to get used to it. I want my fucking cock back. I'm earning my debt back too slowly. What can I do to get my cock back quicker?"

Brittany and Eva glared at Jenni. She realized her mistake. She was lucky enough to be an attractive woman. There was potential for her to sell her body at a higher price than she was charging now. Brittany and Eva's unattractiveness was like a prison. They couldn't charge men to have sex with them and were looking at years as maids before they were free.

But Jenni's body was a prison too. They way men looked at her. The hunger in their eyes carried potential for money but also for danger.

"Don't worry about it," Sheila said. "You've only been here a month. It takes time to build up a client base and a reputation."

"She's right," Nadia said. " You have to work your way up from call girl to high-class call girl who can charge the top amount."

"I'm not looking at this as a career," Jenni said. "I want to know if there's any opportunities for a fast hustle with a big payoff?"

"No," Lucy said firmly.

It was obviously time to drop the subject so Jenni concentrated on her cards. Clarissa put her cards on the table and gave the other ladies the stink eye.

"Come on," she said. "Don't be so hard on Jenni. She's only thinking the same thing we all thought when we first ended up here."

Nadia scratched her breast and sighed.

"Clarissa's right," she said. "We've all tried to find a big payoff. Mr. Jones made sure there wasn't one. Don't you get it? He's not just making us pay off our debt. He's making an example of us to his people. Fuck with him and you lose your balls, literally."

Jenni's heart sank. She didn't know how long she could survive trapped in this body. She was afraid if she stayed this way for too long she would forget how to be Johnny and lose him forever.

"I guess you're right," Jenni said.

After a few more hands, she took a break to go to the bathroom. She closed the bathroom door but didn't lock it. She sat on the toilet and peed. She had just finished and was wiping herself when Lucy slipped in and closed the door behind her. She stood next to Jenni as she washed her hands. She grinned as she looked Jenni over.

"What's up, Lucy?" Jenni said.

"How are you doing on clothes?" Lucy said. "I have a lot of nice things in your size. Why don't you come by my place after the game?"

"I'm doing fine on clothes."

Lucy put her hand on Jenni's stomach and slid it down to her crotch. She cupped Jenni's pussy and gave it a squeeze. Jenni shivered as pleasant sensations spread through her body. She felt her nipples stiffen.

"I miss that sweet pussy of yours," Lucy said. "I'll give you three hundred bucks to go to my place right now."

Jenni pushed Lucy's hand away.

"Is that your three hundred bucks or does it already belong to me?"

Lucy blushed.

"How did you find out?"

"That you paid me for sex with my money? Peter told me."

"I'm sorry. I shouldn't have hustled you."

Jenni laughed.

"Don't worry about it. We're hustlers. It's what we do. Come on. Let's get back to the game."

Jenni started toward the door, but Lucy grabbed her arm.

"What about my offer? This would be my money. No fooling "

"Maybe later."

The door opened and Clarissa came in. She shut the door behind her. The bathroom was crowded with the three of them.

"Are you trying to eat her pussy?" Clarissa said.

"Why not?" Lucy said. "It's almost as sweet as yours."

"I'm not jealous. I came here to talk to Jenni. Alone."

Lucy got the hint and left. Clarissa leaned against the wall and crossed her arms.

"You really serious about making more money?" she asked.

"Hell, yeah," Jenni said.

"I work part time at a strip club. I make decent money on tips and crazy money on lap dances in the V.I.P. room. If you want, I can talk to the manager about getting you a few shifts at the club."

Jenni had gotten used to men paying her money to see her naked, but that was only one guy at a time. She wasn't sure if she could handle a drunken crowd watching her. But if it got her the money she needed, she was willing to try.

"What if the casino finds out?" Jenni said.

Clarissa rolled her eyes.

"Who do you think owns the damn titty bar?" she said.

"Then why aren't the other women dancing there?"

"Everybody has their limits. I'm a hardcore hustler. I do whatever it takes. What about you, Jenni Jones?"

Jenni crossed her arms.

"I'm a hardcore hustler. I'll do whatever it takes to get my cock back."

Chapter Four

Jenni peeked through the curtain at the men sitting at tables and the counter around the stage. They nursed beers and stacks of dollar bills. Considering it was a Wednesday morning, there was a decent crowd watching the half-naked dancer on stage. Watching the muscles on her well-toned body ripple as she did amazing gymnastics on the stripper pole made Jenni nauseous.

Clarissa put her arm around Jenni's shoulder.

"Having second thoughts?" Clarissa said.

"Yes," Jenni admitted. "But I'm not backing out. I can do this."

"That's my girl. Remember. This is your first time. Take it slow. Don't touch the pole. You're not ready. Just swing your hips and shake her tits."

Jenni nodded. Clarissa had explained the procedure. She would be on stage for three songs. Keep her clothes on during the first song. Take off her top during the second song. Take off her bottom during the third song. At the end of the third song, pick up her clothes and her last shred of decency and get the hell off the stage.

She shivered. The air conditioning was turned way up. It was like being in a damn meat locker. Her nipples were so stiff they ached. It didn't help that her stripper outfit barely covered her private parts and left the rest of her bare. Clarissa had tried to talk her into getting her belly button pierced, but pierced ears was as far as Jenni would go.

Getting the job at Doublemint Armadillo was easier than Jenni expected. Clarissa explained that normally there was a dance audition, but since the casino owned the strip club, they hired her on the spot. It wasn't quite that easy. The manager put her on a slow weekday shift.

The dancer before Jenni was winding up her second song. One more song and it would be Jenni's turn. Jenni put her hands on her hips and took deep breaths. Her two-piece outfit was bright pink and sparkly.

"I'm having a problem and I don't how to deal with it," Jenni said.

Clarissa narrowed her eyes at Jenni.

"If you have to pee," Clarissa said, "you still have time to run to the little girl's room."

"It's not that."

"You don't have time to take a crap."

"No. It's not anything like that. It's just...it's just I'm really fucking horny right now."

Clarissa laughed.

"No shit? The idea of dancing naked gets you hot?"

"No. It doesn't. But being backstage with all those dancers, most of them naked and the rest damn near close to it, turned my pussy into a fucking swamp. Their bodies are so perfect. All those perky tits and smooth butts. They smell so nice. I thought being a woman would tamper my desire for pussy, but I was wrong."

Listening to the what the dancers talked about back stage had been an eye-opener for Jenni. The main topics had been child care, graduate school, and real estate.

Clarissa smirked.

"Every man that comes to a titty bar has the same fantasy," she said. "To go backstage where the girls hang out and see them in their natural environment. You got to live the fantasy. You had to become a woman to do it, but you still did it." She pulled back the curtain and pointed at the men in the club. "You know what they're thinking. Use that knowledge. Be the fantasy that you share with them."

Jenni stared at the men. She nodded. Maybe she could pull this off after all.

The third song ended and the dancer gathered her clothes and the dollar bills the men had tossed at her. She left the stage and said hello to Clarissa before heading to the dressing room.

"We have a new girl. This will be her first time on a stage anywhere," the DJ announced. "Give a warm round of applause for Jade."

Jenni hadn't picked the stripper name Jade just as she hadn't chosen the name Jenni. It was chosen for her. She pasted a big smile on her face and sauntered out onto the stage. The first song, also not chosen by her, began to play.

She was almost to the edge of the stage when she slipped and landed hard on her ass. The men laughed. Her face burned with embarrassment. Clarissa pulled the curtain aside and shouted at her.

"Be the fantasy!" she said.

Jenni thought about how Johnny would have reacted if he'd seen a stripper fall on her ass. He wouldn't have cared that she fell as long as she showed him her tits.

Since she was already down, she stayed down. She squirmed on the ground as if she were being fucked, spreading her legs and lifting her ass. She got on her hands and knees and rocked as if she was being taken from behind. She pretended that Keith's big black cock was slamming into her pussy.

She continued her floor show until the end of the first song. She got to her feet for the second song. A couple of the men ambled over to the stage and jammed dollars into her garter belt. Their fingers grazed against her thighs sending tingles to her sopping wet pussy. She resisted the urge to push their faces into her crotch.

Jenni undid her top and let it slide off, freeing her tits. She thought it would bother her to have the men stare at her tits, but that was what this place was for. In fact, she found that it excited her. She squeezed her tits together and smirked at the men before running her hands down her sides. A man wearing madras shirt and tan slacks came to the stage and stuck a ten in her garter belt.

She was a terrible dancer so she avoided moving around too much. She leaned against the stripper pole and squatted down. She desperately wanted to stick her hand inside her panties and play with her pussy. Though she was sure the crowd would enjoy it, she knew it wasn't allowed.

Instead, Jenni straddled the stripper pole. She pressed her crotch against the shiny metal and moved up and down. The pole rubbed against her clitoris in just the right way. She only meant to do this for a moment as a way to excite the crowd, but once she got going she couldn't pull herself away.

Her face flushed as she humped the pole. Men surrounded the stage and made it rain. Dollar bills fluttered around her and soon covered the floor. Jenni held onto the pole and drove herself closer to an orgasm. The lust in the men's eyes and the bulges in their pants turned her on even more.

163

She wasn't sure what she was doing was allowed. Maybe she had stepped over a line. But she was too close to care. A warm feeling in her stomach spread through her body. Her muscles tensed and then an orgasm ripped through her. She convulsed as she ground her crotch against the pole.

Jenni released the pole and took a few unsteady steps away from it. The men wandered back to their seats. She shuffled around the stage as she cooled down.

She panicked when the third song began. When she took off her panties, they would see how wet she was and that her clitoris was sticking out. She was certain the entire bar could smell her pussy.

She had no choice. This was the job. She slipped off her panties and dropped them on top of her bra. A cold wet trail of her pussy juices dripped down her leg and glistened in the spotlight.

Madras shirt and tan slacks man returned to the stage. She squatted down and he put another ten-dollar bill in her garter belt. His hand brushed against her thigh. When he pulled it away, he noticed that it was wet. He gave his hand a quick sniff and grinned at Jenni. She grinned back. If he only knew how much she wanted to suck his cock.

No one else came up to the stage and Jenni managed to make it to the end of the song without jerking off or falling on her ass. With great relief, she retrieved her outfit and gathered her money. Then she rushed off the stage. Clarissa was waiting for her.

"Not bad for your first time," Clarissa said. "But next time, don't fuck the pole. The other dancers hate it when you make it slick."

"I can't believe I just danced naked in front of a room full of strangers," Jenni said. "Fuck! I can't believe I jerked off in front of a room full of strangers."

"It's what we do here for a living. Now get cleaned up and dressed so you get your ass out there."

"I thought it would be a while before it was my turn again."

"We don't just sit back stage between dances. Mingle with the crowd. Thank the men who tipped you. If you're lucky they'll ask you to join them. Then you can talk them into a table dance."

Jenni's eyes widened.

"Shit! I forgot about table dances."

"And lap dances. And trips to the V.I.P. room."

Jenni put her hand on her forehead.

"This is as hard as being an escort."

Clarissa laughed and put her arm around Jenni's shoulder.

"It's just different, that's all. I'll explain how everything works here at the titty bar."

Chapter Five

Jenni did her best to remember who threw money at her while she was on stage. It was such a blur she was certain she'd miss somebody. She didn't really understand why she had to thank them for giving her money. She'd shown them her tits. They should be thanking her.

She definitely remembered madras shirt and tan slacks man. He got some of her pussy juice on his hand. He grinned from ear to ear when he saw her approach his table.

"Thank you for the tip," Jenni said.

"My pleasure," he said. "Would you care to join me?"

Jenni would have preferred to stay backstage and watch the dancers wipe the sweat off their breasts, but mingling with the customers was part of her job.

"I would love to," she said.

Jenni's butt had barely touched the chair next to him when the waitress showed up at their table and asked them if they'd like something to drink. He had hardly touched his frozen Margarita, but he ordered a fresh one and told Jenni to get whatever she wanted.

She ordered a Bourbon and Coke. As a new employee, Jenni wasn't allowed to drink alcohol yet. She knew that the waitress would actually bring her a diet Coke with no alcohol and her new friend would get charged for the missing Bourbon.

"I'm Jade," Jenni said.

"I'm Chester," he said. "Chester Rogers."

"What brings you to Las Vegas, Chester?"

Chester sat up straight and puffed out his chest.

"I'm in town for the World of Concrete. It's the largest international convention of concrete and masonry professionals."

"Sounds heavy."

Chester guffawed.

"Heavy! I get it. Concrete is heavy."

Their drinks arrived and Chester paid the waitress. He was a decent looking fellow. He was fit and had a strong jaw. His cologne was as cheap as his haircut. He was tan except for a pale stripe on his ring finger where he must normally wear his wedding ring.

Jenni struggled to act interested as Chester droned on about the masonry industry. He finally stopped talking long enough to take a sip of his melting Margarita and Jenni took advantage of the opening.

"Would you like a table dance?" Jenni said.

He blushed.

"Yes, I certainly would," he said.

He took out his wallet and gave her twenty dollars.

Jenni went over in her mind the instructions Clarissa had given her for the best way to do a table dance. She waited for the next song to begin. She had Chester scoot his chair so the table wouldn't be in the way. Johnny had gotten enough table dances to know that she didn't actually have to dance on top of the table.

She grabbed Chester's knees and pushed his legs apart so she could stand between them. Then, she smiled at him as she took off her outfit. He blushed every time they made eye contact. Jenni knew that when it came to sex, women had great power over men, but she had no idea how exciting it could feel. Manipulating Chester was making her wet all over again.

She draped her bra and panties over his shoulder. He gazed at her body with naked lust. He may be a boring concrete salesman, but he was a man. They both understood that he wasn't allowed to touch her, but she could touch him. Jenni planned to torture him as much as possible.

She lifted her right breast and licked the nipple. Then she did the same to the left one. She knelt between his legs and blew her hot breath on his crotch. Chester whimpered.

She could see his cock straining at the fabric, desperate to be set free. If only Chester knew about her forced addiction to cock. If only he knew that she wanted his cock inside her as much as he did.

Jenni brushed her breast against his chest and held her nipples inches away from his face. She turned her back to him and rubbed her bare ass against the crotch of his tan slacks. She could feel the outline of his erection.

She continued to tease him until the end of the song.

"Thank you," Jenni said as she reached for her outfit.

"Please," Chester said, scrambling for his wallet. He fished out another twenty and held it out. "One more dance."

Jenni snatched the twenty from his hand.

"Sure," she said.

As the next song played, she rubbed her tits against his chest and her ass against his crotch. She glanced around to make sure no one was watching. She put her hand behind her as she bent down to rub her ass on his crotch again and massaged his cock through his pants. With the combined friction of her ass and her hand, she knew she was driving him wild, but with her back to him, she wasn't sure how close he was to coming.

Chester let out a strangled cry as his hips bucked. Jenni could feel his cock jerking. She had her own small orgasm as she pressed her ass against him.

She stood and looked down at Chester's pants. A large wet was spreading in the center of his crotch. Jenni figured he must have been backed up to produce that much semen. She felt oddly proud of herself for making him release it.

Chester looked like he was going to be sick as he stared at his wet crotch. He pressed his knees together and leaned forward in an unsuccessful attempt to cover his accident. Their waitress swung by, spied Chester's wet spot, winked at Jenni, and walked away without asking if they wanted anything.

"Shit!" he said. "What do I do?"

"Go to your hotel room and change?" Jenni said.

The song hadn't ended, but the dance was obviously over. She retrieved her outfit and began dressing.

"I can't go back to my room," Chester said. "My wife might be there."

"I take it she doesn't know you're here," Jenni said.

"Nobody does. My company thinks I'm spending the day with my wife and my wife thinks I'm at the convention."

Jenni finished dressing and sat in the chair across from Chester. He stuck out his lower lip and tears ran down his face. Jenni took the napkin from under her soda and handed it to him.

"Calm down," she said. "We've all been in this situation some time in our lives. It happened to me when I was a teenager. I was dry humping Sally Gordon, got carried away, and creamed my jeans."

Chester's eyes widened.

"You used to be a guy?"

Jenni frowned. There was no way she could explain how a forced dose of nanobots changed her gender, so she quickly invented a story that was easier to swallow.

"Yeah. Couldn't tell, could you? Amazing what surgery can do."

Chester turned green and his cheeks puffed out. He covered his mouth and managed not to puke his Margarita.

"I deserve this," he said. "I have sinned and God is punishing me."

Jenni rolled her eyes.

"Stop being a whiny bitch," she said. "Here's what you're going to do. Untuck your shirt. That will help hide the spot. Order another drink. Watch the naked girls dancing on stage until your pants dry. There are plenty of men's clothing stores on the strip. I'm sure at least one of them sells tan slacks. Buy new slacks and throw away the stained pair."

Chester's face lit up and mopped his forehead with the napkin.

"That's a brilliant plan," he said.

Jenni leaned forward so he could see plenty of cleavage.

"Then tonight when you're fucking your wife," she said. "Pretend you're fucking me."

Chapter Six

The rest of Jenni's shift went fairly smoothly. She didn't slip on the stage and fall on her ass again and she managed to give table dances without the customers coming in their pants. Plus, she was getting used to walking around half naked. She hardly noticed the guys gawking at her tits.

She went back stage after dancing on stage and noticed the dancers were changing into their street clothes while girls Jenni had never seen before were taking off theirs. Jenni checked her watch and realized that afternoon shift had ended and the evening shift was taking over. She went to her locker to get her clothes. As she was dialing the combination on her lock, someone tapped her shoulder. She turned and saw it was Clarissa. She was still in her stripper outfit.

"Hey, Clarissa," Jenni said. "I really appreciate all your help today. Let me buy you dinner."

"Dinner will have to wait," Clarissa said. "I just got a personal request to entertain a client in a V.I.P. room."

"Okay. Maybe some other time."

"The client wants two girls and left it up to me to pick the second girl. I thought you might want to be her."

Jenni leaned against the locker.

"Remind me how the V.I.P room works," she said.

"The customer can do whatever he wants with the girl as long as he pays her enough," Clarissa said. "The rooms for the regular customers have security cameras supposedly for the dancers' safety, but really the cameras are there so the security guards can watch the dancers fucking. Then there are special room for special clients. Most of them are high rollers, professional athletes, and rich businessmen. There are no security cameras."

Jenni narrowed her eyes at Clarissa.

"No cameras?"

Clarissa nodded.

"Things can get kinky. But those rich bastards love to throw money around. Girl can make some serious money in the special rooms."

"And this client who asked for you. Is he in a special room?"

"Yes, ma'am."

"Anybody I know?"

"You might. How often do you go to the movies?"

"Hardly ever."

"Then you might not know him. Which is probably for the best. You won't be awestruck and forget why we're in there."

Jenni shrugged.

"Count me in."

Clarissa led Jenni through the club and up the stairs to the third floor. Jenni hadn't been to this part of the building before. There was a long hallway with padded doors on either side. Clarissa stopped at the first door on the left. She winked at Jenni.

"Showtime," Clarissa said.

She opened the door and Jenni was almost knocked over by the cloud of marijuana smoke that poured out. The two women entered. The room was bigger than Jenni's entire motel room. There were plush couches, low tables, a wide screen TV, and a wet bar. Four men were sprawled out on the couches. They paused from passing a joint between them to check out Clarissa and Jenni. From the satisfied smiles on their faces, Jenni could tell that they liked what they saw.

One of them stood while the rest stayed seated. He wore an expensive suit with no tie and an open shirt. He had on a gold necklace. His head was shaved. He had a square jaw and sparkling white teeth. He was mixed race. He was so muscular he was about to burst out of his expensive suit. He looked familiar, but Jenni wasn't sure where she'd seen him.

Jenni had been trained to desire all cocks, but it was only recently that she began to notice a man's appearance. And to develop preferences. She liked cute guys with tight asses. She liked tall handsome men who moved with confidence.

Ethnicity didn't matter to her. Hair color meant nothing. She didn't care if a guy worked out or was even a bit soft around the middle but was turned off by fat slobs.

She hated this about herself because it was a sign that she wasn't just a man trapped in a woman's body, but an actual woman with feminine tastes and an attraction to men.

And Jenni was attracted to this man.

"Candi!" he said. "I was beginning to think you forgot about me."

Candi was Clarissa's stripper name.

"I could never forget you," Clarissa said.

He wrapped his big arms around Clarissa and they hugged. They disengaged, but he kept his arm around her waist.

"I asked you to pick the other girl and you didn't disappoint," he said gesturing at Jenni.

"This is my good friend, Jade," Clarissa said. "Jade, this is Rex Rock."

The name rang a bell. He was a movie star. She'd seen him in an action movie but she couldn't remember the plot or the title.

Johnny had played cards with movie stars. He liked playing them because they always lost a lot of money to him and were rarely upset about it.

Jenni held out her hand.

"Pleasure to meet you Mr. Rock," she said.

"Really? Shaking hands?" Rex said. "Bring in here young lady."

Rex let go of Clarissa, grabbed Jenni's hand, and pulled her to him. He hugged her and ground his pelvis against her stomach. He let her go and put an arm around each woman's waist so that they were on either side of him as if they were his own personal harem.

"Candi is the sexiest girl in this whole damn bar," Rex said. "When I asked her to join me tonight, I told to bring the second sexiest girl and damn if she didn't."

"Yeah," Clarissa said. "Jade is pretty fucking sexy."

"Fuck. What we standing around for? Ladies, have a seat. Party with us."

Rex sat on the couch. Clarissa and Jenni sat on either side of him. The men chatted as if the women weren't in the room.

Johnny had been around enough men like Rex in Vegas over the years to know that the three men were Rex's entourage. Their job was to service his ego while pretending to be his friends. Depending on Rex's mood, he might pay Jenni or Clarissa to give one of these guys a blowjob.

They lit up a new joint and passed it around. Whenever the joint came to Clarissa, she took a toke, but when it was Jenni's turn she passed it along. Since this was her first day, she wanted to keep a clear head. It was a fool's errand because there was so much pot smoke in the air that Jenni got a contact high.

Jenni couldn't remember the last time she'd gotten buzzed on pot. She felt warm and fuzzy. She got the giggles. She thought every stupid joke the guys told was hilariously funny. They more she laughed, the more they competed for her attention. They offered to make Jenni a drink from the wet bar, but she turned them down though she never would have imagined that having a group of men flirt with her could be more fun than getting drunk.

Meanwhile, Rex had zeroed in on Clarissa. She had her hand on his leg as he nuzzled her neck. They talked like they'd been dating for months. Maybe they had.

Jenni wasn't sure where the baggie of cocaine came from. Johnny loved cocaine so Jenni loved it too. She caught Clarissa's eye and nodded at the cocaine to see if it was okay if she had some. Clarissa grinned.

"Just save some for me, girl," Clarissa said.

When the guys offered her some blow, she eagerly accepted. The table had a mirrored surface so they laid out the lines on top of it. Rex rolled up a fifty-dollar bill to use as their straw. He handed it to Jenni.

"Ladies first," he said.

Jenni could feel everyone staring at her tits hanging down as she leaned over the table. She put the straw to her right nostril and snorted a row. The rush from the powder exploded in her head. She put the straw to her left nostril and snorted the next row. Her heart was beating a mile a minute as she handed the straw back to Rex.

Everybody took a turn and soon everyone was rubbing their nose and feeling good.

One of the guys, Jenni thought his name was Gerry but she wasn't sure, confessed that he had this fantasy about snorting coke off a stripper's ass. He asked if it was okay if he did it now.

Jenni wasn't sure if he was asking her and Clarissa or Rex for permission.

"If the ladies are willing," Rex said, "then I say go for it. Live the dream."

Clarissa frowned at Jenni, but Jenni shrugged.

"Sure," Jenni said. "Let me get in position."

She climbed over Gerry's lap so that her ass was just below his face. She felt the powder sprinkled on her ass cheeks. She heard loud snorting and then the other guys cheered.

The next thing she knew, Jenni had to let the other three guys snort coke off her ass.

"I think the lady deserves a tip for that," Rex said.

The three men reached for their wallets and each handed Jenni a hundred dollars. She folded the three hundred into her garter belt.

"When are they going to dance?" Gerry said. "I want to see their titties."

Clarissa stood.

"We can listen to the club music in here," she said. "Jade and I can either dance together or one at a time. Your choice."

The guys argued back and forth, but then Rex stood and put his fists on his hips.

"Sorry, boys," he said. "But you have to go now. I want to be alone with the ladies."

Jenni thought sure they'd get pissed off, but then Rex paid these guys to be his friends. They couldn't afford to talk back to him. They made fresh drinks and filed out of the room.

Clarissa put her hand on her hip.

"I see this is going to be a private dance," she said. "Do you want us to dance together or one at a time?"

Rex slipped off his jacket and tossed it on the back of the couch.

"No dancing," he said. "I want to get naked and fuck both of you."

Chapter Seven

Jenni pulled Clarissa aside.

"How does this work?" she said.

"We take off our clothes and fuck this guy," Clarissa said.

"I get that. But what about the rules. Rule number one is we get the money first. No money. No sex. Does that apply here or do we get paid afterwards?"

"Don't worry. He'll give us the money first."

Jenni trusted Clarissa so she took off her outfit. Clarissa did the same. Even though Clarissa had been walking around all day half naked, seeing her completely naked took Jenni's breath away. Her heavy breasts were accented by her reddish-brown nipples. She had a thin waist that flared out into wide luscious hips. Johnny had never been an ass man but then he'd never seen an ass like Clarissa's. It was like two brown volleyballs. Her legs were sturdy and muscular.

Jenni wished so badly that she'd had her cock at that moment. She would have pushed Clarissa to her knees and taken her from behind.

She was getting too turned on by Clarissa. She was here to service a client so she turned her attention to Rex. He was naked. His body was perfect as if he'd spent hours in the gym with a trainer, which Jenni was sure he did. He had a powerful chest, muscular arms and legs, a tight ass, six pack abs, and a very nice cock. It wasn't huge, maybe eight inches at most, but it thick. It was half erect and started to bob in anticipation.

Rex held his pants as he dug into the pocket. He took out a stack of folded bills barely contained with a gold money clip. He licked his thumb before counting out two stacks of money. He gave a stack to each of the women. Jenni quickly counted hers. It was a thousand dollars in one hundred dollar bills. She assumed that Clarissa received the same amount. She put the money with her clothes.

Jenni and Clarissa stood on either side of Rex and pressed their bodies against him. Jenni massaged his balls while Clarissa slowly jerked his cock. He put his hand on their asses and squeezed. He kissed Clarissa and then Jenni, pushing his tongue down her throat. He turned to kiss Clarissa again and Jenni sucked on his nipple.

"I love it when two beautiful women take turns sucking my cock," Rex said.

Clarissa caught Jenni's eye and winked. The two women got on their knees. Rex's cock bobbed between them.

"Who should go first?" Jenni said.

"Age before beauty," Clarissa said.

Jenni grinned. She licked the drop of pre-come off the head of Rex's cock and savored the salty flavor. She took him into her mouth and ran her tongue over the shaft. Rex moaned his approval. She sucked on the head while jerking the shaft.

Clarissa tapped her on the shoulder.

"Mind if I cut in?" Clarissa said.

Jenni pulled away, giggled, and wiped her mouth. Clarissa quickly swallowed Rex's cock all the way down to the root. While Clarissa sucked his cock, Jenni licked his balls.

"This feels so fucking good," Rex said. "I could easily come like this, but I don't want to. Not yet. Get on your hands and knees, side by side."

The floor was covered in plush carpet. Perhaps the Doublemint Armadillo knew that people would be fucking on it and wanted to make it as comfortable as possible. Jenni and Clarissa got on their hands and knees. Rex knelt between them. He slapped their asses and the women yelped in unison.

He slid his hands between their legs and played with their pussies. Jenni gasped at his touch and then mewed happily when his fingers found her clitoris. She looked to the side. Clarissa's eyes were half open as she moaned with pleasure.

On impulse, Jenni leaned over and kissed Clarissa. She froze, thinking that Clarissa would pull away, but instead Clarissa stuck her tongue into Jenni's mouth. Rex pulled his hands away. He pushed Clarissa's legs further apart and licked her pussy. Clarissa moaned with greater intensity as she continued kissing Jenni.

Rex switched from eating Clarissa's pussy to eating Jenni's. Jenni pulled away from Clarissa's lips and pressed her forehead against the floor as erotic pleasure coursed through her body.

"Please," she whimpered. "Put it in."

"What's that?" Rex said. "What do you want?"

"I want you to put your cock in my pussy."

"Beg me."

"Please. Fuck me! Fuck me with your big cock."

Rex answered by pressing the tip of his cock against Jenni's wet pussy. He pushed his thick cock into her, slowly stretching her open. Jenni dug her fingers into the carpet and gritted her teeth. It felt so fucking good. He quickly picked up the pace, slamming into her again and again. Jenni could feel an orgasm building up inside her.

But then, he pulled out of her and she gasped in frustration. She was so close.

Rex moved over to Clarissa who was still on her hands and knees. He felt between her legs.

"Damn girl," he said. "You are so fucking wet."

"You turn me on," Clarissa said.

Rex slipped his cock into Clarissa's pussy. She moaned and pushed her ass back to meet his thrusts. Jenni sat on her knees and watched in amazement as Clarissa's pussy greedily swallowed his cock.

Jenni stood next to Rex and held up her breasts.

"Here," she said. "This will give your mouth something to do."

Rex sucked on Jenni's nipple. Clarissa's magnificent ass bobbed up and down.

"Oh shit!" Clarissa said. "You're making me come."

Rex grabbed Clarissa's ass as she moaned loudly. He pulled out his cock and she collapsed on her stomach. He stroked his slick cock and smiled up at Jenni.

"Your turn," he said. "On your hands and knees."

Jenni was impressed that he didn't come while he was inside Clarissa, but she was glad he hadn't ejaculated yet. She still hadn't come herself.

She got on the floor and Rex positioned himself behind her. Clarissa rolled over on her back and stared at the ceiling. She rubbed her stomach.

"Damn, Rex," she said. "You are something else."

"Hey," Rex said. "You're not done."

Clarissa sat up.

"Where do you want me, boss?" she said.

Rex slapped Jenni's ass.

"Tell me, Jade," he said. "You ever eat pussy?"

Johnny had eaten lots of pussy and considered himself pretty decent at it, but for Jenni the opportunity had never arose. She wondered if she would be any better at it now that she had a pussy herself.

"Yeah," Jenni said. "I've been down on a girl before."

Rex stood.

"Let's get on the couch," he said. "Clarissa, put that sweet pussy where Jade can get to it. I want to watch Jade eat you out while I fuck her from behind."

Clarissa hesitated. The look on her face seemed to say that this wasn't a good idea. But then, she got on her back at the foot of the couch. She spread her legs apart. Jenni got on her stomach between her legs and Rex got bchind her.

"Get on your knees and hike your ass in the air," Rex said.

Jenni did as he instructed. Clarissa's glistening pink pussy was inches from her face. It smelled wonderful. She didn't wait for Rex. She dug her hands under Clarissa and grabbed her glorious ass cheeks. She buried her face between Clarissa's legs and began to lick her pussy lips.

She felt Rex's cock slid easily into her sopping wet pussy. Soon, the three of them developed a rhythm with Rex thrusting into Jenni and Jenni driving her tongue into Clarissa.

Jenni realized that at this moment she was nothing more than a fuck toy whose only purpose was to please these two people. Her nipples brushed against the couch as she gently nibbled Clarissa's clitoris. She ground her pussy against Rex's cock as it grew hotter and hotter inside her. The room filled with their combined fuck smells along with their moans and whimpers.

Clarissa came first. She grabbed Jenni's head and her legs bounced up and down. She screamed oh, oh, oh, but it sounded more like a dog barking. Her eyes rolled back into her head. Jenni lapped up her flowing pussy juices as Clarissa's orgasm ripped through her.

Watching Clarissa must have set off Rex because he came next. He grabbed Jenni's hips and slammed his cock into as hard as he could. She could feel his cock jerked as he filled her with his hot sperm. He growled loudly.

Then finally, Jenni reached the orgasm she'd been denied earlier. It spread from her stomach to her tits to her toes. She moaned into Clarissa's pussy as she came on Rex's cock. She was glad she had been forced to wait because it was the most intense orgasm she'd had since that night in the casino basement when she was first turned into a woman and Mr. Jones' men had gangbanged her for hours.

Rex waited until his cock had grown soft before pulling out of Jenni. Clarissa got up from the couch and made everyone a well-deserved drink. The three of them sat naked on the couch and sipped their drinks as Rex told them about the latest films he'd worked on.

Eventually, they got dressed. Before they left the V.I.P. room, Rex gave each woman a five-hundred-dollar tip.

Chapter Eight

In their street clothes, Jenni and Clarissa looked like typical tourists having dinner at a nice restaurant. No one would guess that an hour earlier they had been having sex with a movie star in the V.I.P. lounge of a famous strip club. And certainly, no one would guess that they were famous male gamblers who had been forcibly turned into women because of the massive debt they each owed a well-known casino.

They were at Momofuku's in the Cosmopolitan Hotel. Their table was filled with small plates, noodle dishes, and ceramic bottles of sake. Back when Jenni was still Johnny, she had loved this place. Eating here made her feel just a teensy bit normal.

She ate slowly while Clarissa attacked the food, jabbing at a bowl and then a plate, and stuffing her mouth.

"What'd I tell you about the V.I.P. rooms?" Clarissa said. "I told you that we could make some decent money in there."

"Is the money always that good?" Jenni said.

Clarissa chewed and swallowed before continuing.

"Most every time I've done it. Sure, once in a while you get one of these celebrities who expects free sex. Mainly rock stars pull that shit because they think all women are groupies."

"Got it. Avoid rock stars."

Clarissa sipped her sake. She put her fork down and put her elbows on the table. She linked her fingers and gazed at Jenni.

"What's wrong?" Jenni said. "You have a strange look in your eye."

"I have a question, but I'm not sure how to ask it," Clarissa said.

"I just had my mouth all up in your pussy. I would think you could ask me just about anything at this point."

"That's part of it."

Jenni looked horrified.

"Should I have not done that? I promise I won't do it again."

"Oh no. That's not the problem. The thing is, that was the best orgasm I've ever had. As a woman."

Jenni felt oddly proud and sat up a little straighter.

"What can I say? It was fun for me too."

Clarissa's eyes lowered to half-mast. If they had been a couple, Jenni would have swooned.

"I didn't think I could feel something like that. We shared something special. At least, I did. And that brings me to my question. I've been trapped in this body longer than you. That means I'll be paying off my debt before you."

"Don't be so sure about that," Jenni said. "I've been hustling pretty hard. I just might pay off my debt sooner than you."

"Well, for argument's sake, let's say I do pay off my first and I get my cock back. By the way, I had a big fucking cock. Much bigger and fatter than Rex's pee shooter."

An image of a big fat cock popped into Jenni's head and she squirmed in her seat.

"Okay. You might get your cock back before me. What's your question?"

The look in Clarissa's eyes told Jenni exactly what she wanted to ask. Jenni's mouth dropped open.

"Would it be okay?" Clarissa said.

Jenni looked around to make sure no one could eavesdrop on their conversation. She leaned forward and spoke in a dramatic whisper.

"You want to know if you can fuck me if you get your cock back before I do?"

"I prefer to think of it as making sweet love," Clarissa said.

Jenni didn't know if she considered Clarissa's request an insult or a compliment. What worried her was that it was more than that. Clarissa felt they had made a connection. For Jenni, it had just been fucking.

"If we had sex as a man and a woman," Jenni said, "I don't know if it would be lovemaking or just fucking."

Clarissa reached over and put her hand on top of Jenni's

"I'll take what I can get," she said.

Jenni glared at Clarissa.

"You'd still have to pay. No money. No sex. That's the rule."

"Don't worry, honey," Clarissa said. "I would definitely pay you top dollar."

Chapter Nine

It was early evening when Logan dropped Jenni off at the motel. She had a bruise on her left butt cheek where she'd fallen on the stage and her feet were killing her from the hours she spent dancing in heels. Though she had brushed her teeth, she still had the taste Clarissa's pussy in her mouth. She was bone tired, but looked forward to going for a swim in the motel pool.

Even before she unlocked the door to room thirteen, she could see the lights were on. Peter was waiting for her. Mr. Jones' money man sat at the table with his legs crossed. He wore his usual sport coat, slacks, dress shirt, and his usual smirk on his face.

Jenni sat on the bed, opened her purse, and handed Peter five rolls of bills. Included in the rolls was the fifteen hundred she'd gotten from Rex Rock. Peter pulled the rubber bands off the first roll and counted the bills. He did the same with the other four rolls. When he was done, he took out a small notebook and pen out of his sport coat pocket, flipped to a page, and noted her latest earnings.

"How close am I?" Jenni asked.

Peter shrugged.

"A lot closer than you were yesterday," he said. "But you still have a way to go. You ran up an enormous debt to the casino."

"I can work tonight. Escort or stripper. It doesn't matter."

"No. Mr. Jones doesn't allow working double shifts. You'll kill yourself and you're no good to us dead."

Jenni didn't care. If she had to be a stripper by day and an escort by night, she would do it. Anything that would pay off her debt sooner. Anything to get her cock back.

Peter put the notebook and pen away.

"You've always been a hell of a hustler," Peter said. "I admire that about you. So, does Mr. Jones."

"Then you know if you hadn't shot me up with those damn nanobots, that as Johnny, I would have found a way to pay off my debt."

"Yeah, probably."

"Then turn me back. I've learned my lesson."

Peter chuckled.

"It doesn't work that way. You have to pay it back according to Mr. Jones' rules."

Jenni felt like she'd been punched in the stomach. Tears welled up in her eyes and she was too exhausted to hold them back. She was working her ass off and didn't feel like she was getting anywhere. Peter pulled two tissues from the tissue box on the desk and handed them to Jenni. She wiped her eyes and blew her nose. He took off his glasses. He pulled out another tissue and used it to wipe the lenses clean.

"I shouldn't be telling you this," Peter said, "but there is a way out of paying your debt to Mr. Jones."

Jenni felt a ray of hope.

"What? Tell me. Whatever it is, I'll do it."

Peter put his glasses back on.

"Pick some night when your purse if full of money from the Johns you fucked and instead of having Logan drive you back here, skip town."

Jenni tilted her head to the side.

"Skip town?"

"That's right. It wouldn't be hard to sneak away from Logan. Go to the bus station and take a bus to any place but Vegas. Then get a fake Social Security card with a new name or better yet, get married and take your husband's last name."

"But you said Mr. Jones would have me killed if I broke the rules."

Peter rolled his eyes.

"There's no rule about skipping town. The rules are to make sure you don't add to your debt. And we keep your cock until you pay off that debt. But it's not worth what it would cost to find you if you ran away."

Jenni took off her heels and massaged her foot.

"But then I'd be stuck this way. I'd never get my cock back."

Peter leaned forward. Jenni noticed he was looking down her dress but she was too tired to care. Let him look at her tits. Just about everybody had already seen them.

"You took to being a woman quicker and better than any gambler we gave the gender swap formula to," Peter said. "I'm sure part of that was because you're a major league hustler and hustlers adapt quickly."

Jenni switched to massaging her other foot.

"I don't know about that," she said. "I still wake up in every morning shocked to find my cock is gone."

"But you make such an outstanding woman," Peter said. "I saw the Doublemint Armadillo's security camera footage of you on stage. You don't dance like a guy in a woman's body. You move like you were born this way. If you say fuck it, I'm going to spend the rest of my life as a hot chick, then you could forget about what you owe Mr. Jones."

Jenni was thankful that there were no cameras in the V.I.P. room because then those assholes would know just how well she fucked as a woman.

"I can't stay this way," she said. "I have to get my cock back."

"The way I see it," Peter said. "Johnny bought more than he can handle and Jenni is stuck paying the bill. If Jenni was smart, she'd say goodbye to Johnny."

"Inside this body, I'm still Johnny. I'll never say goodbye."

Peter tossed the used tissue into the waste basket and stood.

"Hey," he said. "I'm not even supposed to talk about shit like this. But think about it. Jenni."

Peter left the room. Jenni took off her dress. She stood in with her back to the mirror and peered over her shoulder to examine the bruise on her left butt cheek. It was turning purple. She took off her bra and panties and looked at her naked body. She rested her hand on her stomach. Could she really spend the rest of her life like this? She had to admit that there were times when she enjoyed this body even if being a man was easier.

Johnny loved being a man. He loved sliding his cock into a pussy. But Jenni loved having a cock fill up her pussy. She felt a flutter in her stomach from the memory of Rex stretching her open.

Jenni put on her swimsuit, grabbed a towel, her bathing cap, and her room key. She wanted to go for a swim in the motel pool. Swimming helped her organize her thoughts and she had a lot to think about.

The End

GENDER SWAP
GAMBLER 4

Chapter One

Jenni hated Summerlin. It was home of
the richest and most privileged people in Las
Vegas. The last time she'd been here was
when she was still Johnny. He'd gone to a
party for a gaming promoter. The promoter
liked to invite gamblers to his parties because
he thought it made him look cool. It didn't.
As much as Johnny had enjoyed eating the
guy's free food, drinking his free booze, and
staring at his trophy wife's fake tits, he had
been bored him to death and he couldn't wait
to leave.

And now Johnny was back in
Summerlin only this time as Jenni.

She was so used to her clients only
being on the strip that she didn't even
consider that someone might want an escort
out here. Logan parked the car in front of a
typical Summerlin home, a sprawling house
with terracotta roof tiles, palm trees in the
front yard, and adjacent to a golf course.

"Don't look so glum," Logan said. "From what the other girls have told me, these guys typically pay twice as much money and expect half as much sex. Treat this guy right and maybe he'll ask for you again."

Jenni looked at her watch.

"He only booked me for an hour," she said. "Be sure to get back here on time. I don't want to be sitting on his front step waiting on you."

Logan chuckled.

"I'll do my best," he said. "But I can't make any promises."

Jenni swore under her breath and got out of the car. As soon as she slammed the door shut, Logan drove away. He had dropped her off at countless hotels for her to meet clients, this was the first time she felt marooned. She tugged her short dress down, but it still only barely covered her butt. She went to the front door and rang the doorbell. She feared she would be waiting forever for someone to answer but to her relief, the door flew open immediately.

A middle-age man with a bad sunburn and thinning white blond hair stood in the doorway. He wore plaid pants and a polo shirt and had a cigar n his hand. Jenni shrugged. She'd had worst looking clients.

He grinned ear to ear as he looked her over.

"You're perfect!" he said. "I asked for beautiful and that's what they sent me. Come on in."

Jenni didn't mind a compliment now and again. She stepped inside. He led her into a spacious living room filled with expensive furniture.

"My name's Blake," he said. "I forgot what the agency said your name was."

"Jenni."

"Once a month me and my buddies get together for poker. You ever play poker?"

Jenni took a deep breath. Mr. Jones had given her three rules to follow. The most important was rule number three. Never gamble.

"No," she lied. "I don't play poker."

"Really," Blake said. "For some reason, I thought you would. Where was I? Right. Me and the buddies are in the rec room playing poker. For real money. We're serious. We don't fuck around. The wife doesn't like to be around when I have the game here because we smoke cigars, drink like fish, and eat crappy food. She spends the night at a local hotel."

Jenni put her hand on her hip.

"How many guys are here for the game?"

"Five, including me."

"That's going to cost you extra. I don't do group rates."

Blake narrowed his eyes at her and then he laughed.

"I'm sorry," he said. "My bad. I don't want you to do us. Don't get me wrong. I would love to do you, but that's not why you're here. You see, normally the wife takes the kid with her, but this time I insisted that he stay. I mean he's fucking eighteen. I say it's time. Right?"

Jenni crossed her arms. This guy was making absolutely no sense at all. But then the penny dropped.

"I get it," she said. "Your son's a virgin and you want me to pop his cherry."

"Exactly! You'd think he would have figured it out on his own, but the kid's not too bright. Takes after his mother."

Jenni thought it over. The boy was eighteen, so she wouldn't be screwing an underage kid. Since he was virgin, he'd probably come quickly.

"Will you be paying me, or do you want him to do it?" she said.

"You are kidding me?" Blake said. "I wouldn't trust that kid to piss on his own leg."

Blake stuck his cigar in his mouth and chewed on it as he fished his wallet out of his back pocket. He handed Jenni six hundred dollars. She counted it, folded it in half, and stuck the money in her pink purse. She figured that this would be the easiest money she'd make all night.

They climbed the stairs to the second floor. They stopped outside a door with a sign that read, "Danger. Keep Out." Rap music leaked through the door. Blake banged on the door.

"Open the fucking door," he shouted. "She's here."

"I don't want to see her!" shouted the person inside. "Tell her to go away."

"She's a real hot babe with great tits."

"Yeah, right!"

Blake tried opening the door, but it was locked.

"Come on, Shane. That was two years ago. Open the door."

"No! Go away!"

Blake went to the end of the hallway and motioned for Jenni to join him. He leaned in close and she got a good whiff of his rancid cigar.

"I tried to get him laid when he was sixteen," Blake said. "I called your agency. It's got a great reputation, so I didn't bother to specify what kind of girl to send. This girl shows up and she's bit of a plain Jane, but she wasn't a total skank. She certainly couldn't hold a candle to you."

"I'm guessing Shane didn't care for her," Jenni said.

"He bawled like a fucking baby. Said she was the ugliest woman he'd ever seen. Claimed the experience traumatized him and that's why he's still a virgin."

"Damn. That's harsh."

"Like I said, he takes after his mother."

Blake went back to his son's door and banged on it some more. Inside the room, the Rap music got louder. Jenni glanced at her watch. She wanted to get this over with and go back to the strip and guys who weren't traumatized by pussy. She walked over to the door.

"Let me try talking to him," Jenni said. "If I can't get him to let me in, then you'll get your money back."

Blake shrugged.

"Sure. Go ahead," he said.

"Maybe you should leave us alone."

Blake stared at Shane's door and then shook his head.

"Good luck. I'll be downstairs in the den if you need me."

Jenni waited until Blake had descended the stairs. Then she knocked on the door.

"Hey, Shane," she said. "I'm the escort you daddy paid for. My name's Jenni."

The music turned off.

"I'm not interested," Shane said.

"You dad told me how you got burned last time," Jenni said. "I understand. I don't like getting ripped off either. You want the product as advertised."

"Damn right!"

"You won't know if I'm the real deal unless you see me."

"I'm not opening the door. You're trying to trick me."

Jenni couldn't believe she was working this hard to please this little shit.

"I'll make a deal with you," she said. "I'm going to slip the money your dad gave me under the door. Then I want you to open the door. If you like what you see, then you give me the money and I come inside and rock your world. If I don't meet your expectations, then close the door and keep the money. Deal?"

She waited for a minute.

"Okay," Shane said. "Deal."

Jenni took the money Blake had given her. She peeled off two hundred and put the rest back in her purse. She slipped the money under the door. She heard bills crinkling and then the door unlocking. The door cracked open just enough for the kid to peek out. Jenni struck a sexy pose in the hallway.

The door opened all the way. A teenager with spiky blond hair and a smattering of acne on his forehead stared at Jenni. He had blue eyes and was on the thin side. If he dumped the spoiled rich boy pout he wouldn't be bad looking. In fact, he was cute enough that Jenni was surprised some spoiled rich girl his age hadn't already popped his cherry.

His hand trembled as he handed her the two hundred. Jenni smirked as she entered his room.

Chapter Two

Jenni could tell Shane wasn't expecting company. His room was a mess. The bed was unmade, clothes were strewn everywhere, a video game console rested on the floor in front of a TV, posters of hot girls in teeny tiny bikinis hung crooked on the wall, and an electric guitar was gathering dust in the corner. The smell of Axe Body Spray competed with the stench of body odor and cold pizza.

Shane stood in the corner nervously putting his hands in his pockets and then taking them out to cross his arms and then putting them back into his pockets. Jenni could feel him watching her every move. She must have seemed like a rare and exotic animal that had stumbled into his lair. put her pink purse on a desk next to a bong. She slipped off her high heels. She turned her back to him and lifted up her hair.

"Unzip me," she said.

Shane's hands shook as he unzipped her dress. Jenni peeled off her dress. She still had on her bra and panties. She gazed down at Shane's crotch. His boner was about to burst out of his skinny jeans.

"You might want to take your clothes off too," she said. "It's a lot more fun if we're both naked."

Shane turned away from Jenni and quickly shed his clothes. He dashed into the bed and covered himself with a sheet before Jenni could get a good look at him. Jenni took off her bra and panties and got under the covers with him.

She rubbed against him and put her hand on his stomach. She inched her hand down and had almost reached his cock when Shane made the horrified O face of a boy having a premature ejaculation. Which might be the real reason why he was still a virgin.

"That's never happened before," Shane said, tears welling up in his eyes. "It's just you're so fucking beautiful and I was so fucking nervous. I'm such a fucking idiot. You should just leave. Keep the money. Just leave. Okay?"

Jenni was tempted to leave. She had her money. But she couldn't leave him like this. She didn't have the heart. She didn't know why but ever since she'd been turned into a woman, she'd had more empathy for others. She didn't think it had nothing to do with being a female. She knew plenty of heartless women.

"It's okay, Shane," Jenni cooed. "It happens to lots of guys, especially virgins. I'm not going anywhere so just relax." Shane took a deep breath and wiped away his tears. "Where can I get a towel?"

Shane pointed at a door on the other side of the room. Jenni got out of bed and opened the door. He had his own bathroom. She couldn't believe it. The spoiled brat had his own private bathroom. Jenni ignored the porn magazines stacked next to the toilet and snatched a towel off a hook. She came back to the bed and gently lifted the bedsheet to reveal Shane's skinny body.

She had to peel the bedsheet off his crotch. His midsection was covered in sperm. Jenni was impressed. She had never seen so much sperm. Shane laid his head back on a pillow and covered his eyes with his forearm. Jenni used the towel to wipe the sperm off him. She purposely let her hand grazed his cock and it twitched. Just as she suspected. He was a teenage boy. It wouldn't take much to get him hard again.

Jenni tossed the towel aside. She went to her purse and got a condom and a small bottle of lube. Shane still had his eyes covered, so she quickly squirted lube into her hand and lubricated her pussy. She put the lube away and returned to the bed with the condom.

"I happen to know a lot about boys your age," Jenni said. She didn't mention that she used to be one herself because he was upset and confused enough. "They're cocks are very sensitive. That's both a good thing and a bad thing. It's a good thing because they feel everything intensely." Jenni grazed her fingernails along the edge of his shaft. Shane sucked in air. "It's a bad thing because they're cocks are too sensitive, and they end up coming too soon."

Shane put his forearm down and looked at Jenni.

"What should I do?" he said.

Jenni held up the condom.

"Wear a condom," she said. "I suggest the thinnest one you can find. The condom deadens the feeling enough that you don't come right away."

Shane reached for the condom, but Jenni pulled her hand away.

"Not yet," she said. "There's no rush. We'll wait until you're ready and then I'll put it on for you."

"Okay," Shane said.

Jenni was oddly proud of herself. Shane was doing whatever she told him to do.

It was if she had trained a disobedient dog to behave.

"Do you like my tits?" she said.

Shane stared at her tits.

"Yes," he said. "They're fucking beautiful."

"Would you like to touch them?"

"Do you want me to?"

"Yes. I want you to feel my tits."

Shane squeezed her tits and pinched her nipples. He was a little rough, but Jenni enjoyed it. His hands were sending nice signals to her pussy.

"Suck on my nipples," Jenni said.

Shane clamped his mouth on her tit and sucked on her nipple. She could feel it getting hard as a pencil eraser. She ran her hand through his hair and immediately regretted it. He wore twice as much hair gel as she did.

Without having to tell him, he explored her body with his hands. He ran them down her curves, over her ass, along her legs, and across her stomach. Finally, he reached down between her legs. He had no idea what to do with her pussy and wouldn't find her clitoris without a map, but Jenni appreciated his enthusiasm.

She reached down between his legs. His cock was rock hard. She pushed him onto his back and tore open the package. She slipped the condom onto his trembling cock.

Jenni straddled Shane and guided his cock to her pussy. He gasped as she lowered herself onto him.

"Relax," Jenni said. "Take deep breaths. Enjoy the moment."

Shane nodded and smiled. Jenni put her hands on his chest and moved slowly.

"Your pussy feels so fucking good," Shane said.

"So, does your cock," Jenni said. "Hey, guess what, Shane?"

"What?"

"You're not a virgin anymore."

Jenni wished she had a photo of the look of relief and pride on Shane's face. She would have had it framed and given to Blake.

She increased her speed as she rode Shane's cock. He grabbed her tits and pinched her nipples. He held on for three minutes before he filled the condom with his hot come which was pretty damn good for an amateur.

"Feel better now?" Jenni said.

"That was amazing," Shane said. "Did you come?"

"I sure did," Jenni lied.

She climbed off of Shane and removed the condom for him. He'd really filled it up. It was amazing how much sperm teenage boys produced. She tossed it into an otherwise empty wastebasket.

Jenni went into the bathroom and cleaned up. When she came out, Shane was asleep. Typical man. She got dressed and left his room, closing the door quietly behind her.

Chapter Three

Jenni checked her watch as she walked down the stairs. Logan should be coming to pick her up soon. She went into the living room and peeked outside. His car hadn't arrived yet. She was thirsty. She went into the kitchen to see if maybe there was a bottle of water in the frig.

As luck would have it, there was a whole case of bottled water in the frig. Jenni took one out and held it to her cheek. The coolness felt nice on her skin. There was a door at the other end of the kitchen. Jenni heard voices coming from that direction. That must be where Blake and his buddies played cards.

Jenni felt the familiar itch in her hands, the desire to hold the cards and play poker. But she couldn't gamble. That was Mr. Jones' third rule. Never gamble. Not for money. Mr. Jones' bodyguard, Viktor Olav, made it clear to her that he would gladly put a bullet in her head if she ever broke that rule.

But that didn't mean she couldn't watch other people play poker. As long as she didn't join them, she wasn't breaking any rules. Logan would be here any minute, so she'd only have time for a quick peek. There was nothing wrong with a quick peek.

Jenni slunk quietly to the door and peered inside the room. Five men sat at a round table. A cloud of smoke hung over them. They were playing poker. A thrill rushed through her that was as strong as an orgasm. She was tempted to masturbate while she watched them and had to resist reaching for her pussy.

They were too absorbed in the game to notice her spying on them. They laughed and chatted as they played. She picked out Blake's voice. He sounded happy. He would be even happier later when he found out that his son was no longer a virgin.

Jenni recognized another voice. It was a deep voice, as deep as a man's voice, but it was clearly a woman's voice. She sought out the source of the voice and when she located the person an icy chill replaced the erotic charge she'd been getting from watching the game.

It was Brittany Jones. She sat next to Blake. She wore her usual velour track suit. She had more money piled in front of her than any of the other players.

Jenni's stomach churned. Brittany was playing poker. For money. She was bound by the same rules as Jenni. If Mr. Jones found out, he would have her killed. A bullet to the head.

Jenni stumbled away from the doorway and hurried to the front door. She stepped outside, leaned over, and sucked in the cool night air as she waited for a wave of nausea to pass. A car horn startled her. It was Logan.

"Come on," he said. "We have to get back to the strip. Clients are waiting."

Jenni hopped into the back seat. Logan drove away from the house. Jenni took a tissue from her purse and mopped her sweaty forehead. Logan peered at her reflection in the rear-view mirror.

"You okay?" he said. "You're not going to puke in my car, are you?"

Jenni realized she still had the bottle of water in her hand. She twisted off the cap and took a long sip.

"I'm fine," she said. "Nothing to worry about."

"If you say so," Logan said. "You look like you saw a ghost."

Jenni stared out the window.

"I didn't see anything," she said. "Not a goddamn thing."

Chapter Four

Jenni knocked on the door to room thirty-nine. Nobody answered. She knocked again. Still, nobody answered. She banged on the door with her fist. Brittany cracked open the door and peeked out at Jenni.

"What the fuck?" Brittany said.

"We need to talk," Jenni said.

"Later."

"No. Now."

Brittany opened the door the rest of the way. Jenni stepped inside the apartment. Brittany wore a T-shirt and boxer shorts. With her messy short hair, hairy legs, and shapeless body, she could have been mistaken for a man.

"What's so fucking urgent?" Brittany said.

"I saw you last night," Jenni said.

Brittany stared at Jenni.

"Where?"

"Blake's house. I don't remember his last name."

As if on cue, Blake entered the living room from the bedroom. He wore a pink bathrobe. His thinning blond hair stuck out in different directions.

"Is everything okay?" he asked.

"Everything's cool, sugar," Brittany said.

She hustled over to the bedroom door. She gently pushed Blake into the bedroom and closed the door. While she waited, Jenni looked around the living room. The place was a mess. Again. Jenni knew that myth that women were naturally cleaner than men was just that a myth. Johnny's ex-wife Marsha was incapable of cleaning up after herself much less keep an entire house clean. That was why they had hired a maid service to come twice a month.

Brittany emerged from the bedroom. She had replaced her boxer shorts with a pair of pajama pants.

"Let's talk outside," she said.

They left the apartment and sat on lounge chairs by the pool. Sunbeams danced on the green water.

"You're fucking Blake?" Jenni said.

"I have needs," Brittany said. "I would have stayed at his place, but Blake was afraid his wife might come home early. The bitch doesn't care if Blake sees other women, she just doesn't like to find them in her bed and Blake can't afford another divorce."

They watched the pool in silence. Brittany turned to Jenni.

"What did you see?" Brittany said.

"You were gambling," Jenni said. "It looked like you were doing pretty good."

Brittany leaned back in her chair.

"Those guys are amateurs," she said. "I take in a good haul, but I make a point to lose a few hands or else they wouldn't keep inviting me back."

Jenni did a double take.

"How long have you been playing these guys?"

Brittany gazed at the sky as she did the math in her head.

"It's been a couple of years now," she said. "The first time I went over there, Mr. Jones was still making me work as an escort. Blake hired me to fuck his kid, but when he saw me he started crying and said I was an ugly ass whore."

Jenni got it now. Brittany was the escort that "traumatized" Shane when he was sixteen.

"That's harsh," Jenni said.

Brittany shrugged.

"I know I'm an ugly broad, but I didn't need some spoiled brat to scream it in my face. Blake felt bad about the whole thing and offered me a drink. I saw that he and his buddies were playing cards, so I asked if I could sit in for a couple of hands. Those guys are so old school that they were amazed that a woman could play cards as well as a man. They loved having me play with them, so they kept inviting me back."

"When did you and Blake start hooking up?"

"Same night his kid had a temper tantrum. Blake didn't want to get nothing for the money he paid me, so he had me give him a blow job. Turns out we have chemistry."

"But Brittany, what about the rules?"

Brittany rolled her eyes.

"Rule number three," she said. "No gambling. Get caught gambling and you get a bullet in the head."

"Damn right," Jenni said. "I had Viktor Orlov remind me of rule number three. He said it was his job to pull the trigger and you know how much that asshole hates us."

"Rent told you that? I don't believe he was ever in the Russian Mafia. He's never done a hit on anybody. He's full of bullshit."

"But Mr. Jones isn't full of bullshit and these are his rules."

"That's also bullshit. Mr. Jones doesn't give a fuck how I make my nut as long as he gets his money back. I'll be damned if I break my back as a fucking maid for five years to get my dick back. Thanks to my sugar daddy Blake I'll be able to pay off my debt by the end of this year."

"If Mr. Jones doesn't give a fuck how we repay him then why come up with the rules?"

"He just doesn't want us gambling in the casinos."

Jenni thought it over. It didn't add up. If Mr. Jones was crazy enough to turn indebted gamblers into escorts, then it seemed logical that he wouldn't hesitate to kill any escort who got out of line. As women, the gamblers didn't really exist. If their bodies were found, they would be listed as Jane Does.

Jenni loved Brittany but becoming a woman hadn't changed her stubbornness. When Brian made up his mind about something, nothing Johnny told him would convince him that he was wrong. Jenni knew nothing she said to Brittany would make any difference. But she had to try anyway.

"If you're not worried about Mr. Jones' rules, then why are we talking out here instead of in your apartment?" Jenni said.

"Blake doesn't know who I really am," Brittany said. "Not that he would believe me. But why muddy the waters when things are going so well?"

Jenni stood. She wanted to get a swim in before she went to bed.

"You're my best friend," she said. "Please stop gambling."

Brittany stood.

"You worry too much," she said.

Jenni headed toward her room while Brittany headed toward her apartment. Jenni stopped and turned. She watched Brittany enter her apartment. She hoped she was wrong and that Brittany's life wasn't in danger. But she couldn't shake the feeling that she was right.

Chapter Five

A week later, Jenni was back in Summerlin. As Logan followed his GPS through a maze of neighborhood streets, Jenni stared out the car window at what she called show-me-your-wallet houses.

"Did the client really ask for me for by name?" Jenni said.

"That's what the front office told me," Logan said.

Neither Jenni or Logan had ever been to the escort service's offices. They had no idea where it was located. What they did know what that the company was called Anytime Anywhere Escorts, that it was secretly owned by the casino, and that they would call Logan and tell him which girl to take where.

Jenni wondered if she was going back to Blake's house. Maybe Shane wanted to see her again. But that didn't make sense to Jenni. She could see Blake paying for Shane to lose his virginity, but he didn't seem the type to waste money getting his son laid every time he was horny. Blake would expect his son to find his own pussy.

There was also the chance that Blake wanted to see Jenni because she knew he was fucking Brittany. Maybe he wanted to make sure Jenni wouldn't tell anyone about them. He might even want to pay for Jenni's silence.

If that were the case, then Jenni would let him know that she had no intention of telling anyone about Blake and Brittany. Because of Jenni's friendship with Brittany, Blake would be getting Jenni's silence for free.

But then, Logan turned in the opposite direction from Blake's neighborhood. They entered a fancy subdivision. The houses they passed were familiar to Jenni. Too fucking familiar. The acids in her stomach churned and she broke out in a nervous sweat.

Certainly, this was just a coincidence. They couldn't possibly be going where she thought they were going. Her heart beat faster as Logan got closer and closer to the last place in Summerlin she ever wanted to go and the real reason why she despised this neighborhood.

They arrived at a beautiful two-story house with a manicured lawn. Two cars were parked in the driveway. A new BMW and a beat-up Toyota. Logan parked at the curb.

"Is this some kind of sick joke?" Jenni said. "Nobody in this house asked for me."

Logan twisted around and rested his arm on the seat. He tilted his head to the side.

"Why are you being such a whiny bitch?" he said. "I thought you'd be happy that someone out here had asked for you. They have the potential of becoming regular clients. Once you build up a client base you can start charging three times what you're getting now."

"Don't play games with me," Jenni said. "You know damn well that this is my fucking house!"

Logan looked at the house.

"No shit?" he said. "You used to live here?"

"As if you didn't know," Jenni said. "This is one of the three houses I used to own. I sold the others, but my ex-wife got this one as part of our divorce settlement."

Logan took out a cigarette and lit it up. He exhaled, and the car filled with smoke. Jenni tried to wave it away, but her effort accomplished nothing.

"How do you know she didn't sell it?" Logan said.

"Marsha loves this fucking house," Jenni said.

"She might not have had a choice."

Jenni rubbed her forehead. The smoke and the anxiety were giving her a headache.

"You knew this was my house," Jenni said.

Logan lowered the window and tapped the ashes onto the street.

"How would I know this used to be your house?" he said. "It's not like you ever invited Laura over to hang out."

Logan had a good point. The only gambler Johnny ever had over to the house was Brian and that was rare. He preferred to hang out with his friends at a bar, which he did often. It was one of the many reasons why Marsha divorced him.

"I can't go in there," Jenni said. "I can't take the chance that Marsha is in there."

Logan twisted around in the seat again.

"Let's look at this logically," he said. "Your ex-wife doesn't know what happened to you. How in the hell could she ask for you by name?" Jenni was about to argue, but Logan held up his finger to shush her and continued. "Was your ex-wife into muff diving? If not, then why would she order a female escort instead of a male escort?"

Jenni rubbed her forehead again. The headache wasn't going away.

"Last I heard she wasn't into women," Jenni said.

"Did she remarry?" Logan said.

"Fuck no. She would have told me just to rub it in."

"If you look at this logically, then it's highly likely that your ex-wife doesn't live here anymore and that some rich lonely divorcee is in there waiting to pay top price to get his dick wet."

Jenni peered at the house. The curtains were pulled shut. She didn't know if they were the same curtains from when Johnny lived there. He never paid attention to shit like curtains. She had to take a chance that Logan was right, and that Marsha wasn't inside.

She got out of the car and Logan drove away. Her legs were rubbery as she walked up to the front door. She stood on the stoop and pulled her short dress down, but it still only barely covered her ass. She rang the doorbell.

The person who answered the door wasn't Marsha.

It was Keith.

The same Keith who worked for Mr. Jones. The same Keith who helped gangbang Jenni in the casino's basement. The same Keith whose big black cock finally broke Jenni's resistance and got her hooked on all men's cocks.

Yeah. That Keith.

Chapter Six

"What are you waiting for?" Keith said. "Come on in."

He held open the door. Jenni glanced back at the street. Logan's car was gone. Unless she planned to hike miles back to the Moonbeam Motor Lodge in high heels, she was trapped here.

She entered the house and almost fainted. It was exactly as the same as Johnny had left it. The same furniture, the same rugs, and the same artwork hanging on the wall. If all this was the same, then that could only mean one thing.

Marsha still lived here.

Johnny's ex-wife, Marsha, entered the living room. Jenni had forgotten how beautiful she was. Marsha was a tall redhead with high breasts and full hips. She had a girl next-door open face complete with freckles that hid her street smarts and toughness. Marsha smiled showing her gums.

"Oh my God, Keith," Marsha said. "She's gorgeous."

Jenni blushed.

"Didn't I tell you?" Keith said. "I told you the girl was going to be a knockout."

Marsha held out her hand.

"Hi," she said. "I'm Marsha."

"Jenni."

The women shook hands. Marsha's warm skin sent an electric jolt through Jenni. This was beyond surreal. Jenni wouldn't have been surprised if a unicorn showed up with a six-pack of beer.

"I'm Keith," Keith said.

He held out his hand. Jenni reluctantly took it and he gave her hand a strong squeeze while staring into her eyes.

Marsha and Keith were dressed casually in shorts and short-sleeve shirts. Marsha was barefoot.

"I can tell that we're going to have a lot of fun together," Marsha said.

"That's what I'm here for," Jenni said.

Jenni glared at Keith, but he ignored her.

"Should we have something to drink?" Keith said. "Or go straight to the bedroom?"

Marsha playfully punched Keith's arm.

"Don't rush it," Marsha said. "We booked her for the entire night."

Jenni had completely forgotten that she was booked for the entire night. She didn't think she could handle being here that long. She felt that any second she would lose her cool and run screaming from the house.

"You're right," Keith said. "Let's take our time and enjoy ourselves."

Jenni was dying inside, but she kept a smile plastered on her face. If ever she needed Johnny's legendary cool under pressure, this was it. She would handle this the way he would have; by doing whatever was necessary to survive.

"We should get business out of the way first," Jenni said.

"You're absolutely right," Marsha said.

She dashed into the kitchen and returned with her wallet. Jenni wondered why Keith wasn't paying for this since this was obviously his idea. Marsha handed Jenni a roll of money. Jenni counted two thousand dollars. She put it in her pink purse and snapped it shut.

"I believe somebody said something about an adult beverage," Jenni said.

Marsha laughed.

"That's what my ex-husband always called alcoholic drinks," she said. "Adult beverages."

"What's your poison?" Keith said.

"Gin and tonic," Marsha said.

"Bourbon and soda," Jenni said.

"My ex-husband always drank Bourbon and soda," Marsha said.

"We'll see if she sucks dick like your ex-husband," Keith said.

"Keith! That was rude."

"Sorry."

Marsha and Keith laughed. Jenni's cheeks burned as she struggled to keep her smile plastered on her face.

Marsha and Jenni sat together on a couch in the living room while Keith went to the kitchen make the drinks. Jenni looked around the room. On the wall over the couch was a LeRoy Neiman print. It was a painting of a tiger. Johnny hated that painting, but Marsha had to have it.

"You have a lovely home," Jenni said.

"Thank you," Marsha said.

"Have you and Keith lived here long?"

"Keith doesn't live here. Well, he practically lives here since he's stays over all the time, but I own the house. Been here for about six years."

Keith returned carrying two glasses and a bottle of beer. He handed the women their drinks and took a swig from his bottle of beer. He sat in a chair across from the couch.

Jenni sipped her drink. Keith had poured the Bourbon with a heavy hand. Marsha sipped her drink and then placed her glass on the coffee table. She wrapped her legs under her and put her arm on the back of the couch. Her hand was close enough to Jenni that she could touch her.

"Do you mind if I ask you a personal question?" Marsha said.

Jenni took a nervous sip of her drink before putting it down on the table. She hoped Marsha didn't notice how much her hand trembled.

"Not at all," Jenni said.

"Have you ever done this before?" Marsha said.

"You're not my first clients."

"I'm sorry. That's not what I meant. Have you ever been part of a threesome before?"

Jenni took another sip of her drink. "Yes, I have."

"With two women and one man?"

"Yes."

"What about two men and one woman?"

"Do you mean have I been double penetrated?" Jenni glanced quickly at Keith. "Yes, I have."

Jenni was astonished to realize that though she'd only been a woman and an escort for a few months, she had experienced a vast variety of sex with both men and women.

"Wow," Marsha. "I don't mind admitting that I'm a little jealous."

"Don't be," Jenni said. "It's because I'm an escort. We need to be willing to do just about anything."

"Glad to hear that," Keith said.

Marsha and Jenni glared at Keith. He drank his beer.

"When Keith first suggested bringing in another woman, I wasn't sure what to think," Marsha said. "I mean, I should be enough for him, right?"

"You seem like you would be enough woman for anybody," Jenni said.

Marsha blushed. Jenni liked how Marsha's freckles stood out when she blushed.

"But the more I thought about it," Marsha said. "The more excited I got. You see, I've never been with a woman before. I've always been curious about it, but never had the nerve."

Johnny had suggested a few slightly kinky things like this to spice up their marriage, but Marsha had flat out refused. Her refusal wasn't the reason they got divorced, just one more obstacle to them staying together. But now, Marsha was practically gushing about having another woman in her bed. Jenni wondered just what the hell Keith had said to talk Marsha into this impending ménage à trois.

Jenni could certainly understand why Keith wanted to add a second woman. Every heterosexual man dreamed of having two women at the same time.

Keith could have had any escort come here today. Vegas was crawling with escorts. He could have asked for any of the other gamblers turned into escorts. But he had specifically asked for Jenni.

Jenni could think of only one reason why. Keith was being a dick. He wanted Johnny to know that he was fucking his ex-wife. And if that weren't enough of dick move, he was going to make Johnny watch him fuck Marsha while fucking Johnny/Jenni at the same time. He was pulling a major dick move on the man who had lost his dick. What a fucking dick!

And the worse part was that Jenni was going to let him do it because deep down she desperately wanted Keith's cock. She sometimes fantasized about him fucking her the way he did in the basement with his big black cock relentlessly driving her to one orgasm after another.

And then, there were times when she thought about Marsha. It was Johnny's fault that their marriage turned to shit. There were times when he missed her and that meant there were times when Jenni missed her.

As if this sick and fucked up situation wasn't sick and fucked up enough, Jenni wanted to fuck both of them.

"Now you get to find out what it's like to be with a woman," Jenni said.

She leaned over and kissed Marsha lightly on her lips. Marsha jumped back and touched her lips as if she'd gotten an electric shock. She smiled and leaned toward Jenni. At first, they just pressed their lips together, but then Marsha slipped her tongue into Jenni's mouth. Jenni closed her eyes. She didn't want to touch Marsha's breasts too quickly but then she felt Marsha's hands on her breasts.

Marsha cupped Jenni's left breast and then her curious fingers found her nipple. She rubbed her thumb over it, causing wonderful sensations to course through Jenni's body. Jenni put her hand on Marsha's thigh and then moved it between her legs. She could feel the heat from Marsha's pussy through her shorts.

"Hey," Keith said. "What about me?"

Marsha pulled away and laughed. She pushed a strand of Jenni's hair behind Jenni's ear.

"That was nice," she said. "So nice I completely forgot about my boyfriend."

"We could always send him home," Jenni said. "You paid me, so you get to decide."

Marsha grinned.

"I want him to stay," she said. "I want to watch him fuck you."

Jenni felt heat coming from her own pussy.

Keith downed his beer and slammed the bottle on the coffee table. He stood. His erection was clearly visible pressing against the fabric of his shorts.

"Now are we ready to go to the bedroom?" he said.

Chapter Seven

Jenni prayed that Marsha had redecorated the bedroom. She didn't think she could handle having sex in the exact same bedroom and the exact same bed that Johnny used to share with Marsha when they were married. Sure, it was the same bedroom, but hopefully Marsha had made some changes since Johnny moved out.

Jenni felt a mixture of relief and regret when she saw that Marsha had indeed made significant changes. She had replaced the Queen bed with a King, which called for a new set of sheets and blankets. The TV was missing. There was a new rug on the floor. However, the dresser and vanity table were the same and the artwork hadn't changed. Jenni was relieved that it wasn't exactly the same, but she regretted seeing that the main things that had been taken out were any signs that Johnny had ever lived here.

Keith stripped out of his clothes so quickly that he was naked before the women were half way undressed. He stared at them with a goofy smile and his large cock bobbing. Marsha gave him a playful tug.

"Get on the bed, honey," she said. "We'll be with you in a minute."

Jenni turned her back to Marsha and lifted her hair.

"Would you unzip me?" she said.

Marsha leaned in and kissed the back of Jenni's neck. Johnny used to do that to Marsha because she said she enjoyed it. Jenni now understood why. The kiss sent shivers all the way down her spine. The sound of Marsha pulling Jenni's zipper down sent another shiver.

Jenni peeled off her short dress. Along with a bra and panties, she wore black nylons held up with a garter belt. The nylons and garter belt were Lucy's suggestion. Lucy said it turned me on to fuck a woman wearing them. According to Lucy, the garter belt straps emphasized the magnificence of Jenni's ass. Jenni took off her bra and panties, and slipped off her high heels, but she kept the garter belt and nylons on.

Marsha took off her clothes and gave Jenni a naked hug. Their breasts pressed together. Marsha put her hand behind Jenni's head and pulled her in for a kiss. Jenni stole a glance at the bed. Keith leaned against the headboard and stroked himself as he watched the women make out.

Marsha's hands explored Jenni's ass, squeezing the cheeks before giving her a playful smack. Jenni returned the favor by pinching Marsha's ass. Then she pinched Marsha's nipples.

"I still can't believe I'm going to share my boyfriend with another woman," Marsha said.

"I still can't believe your boyfriend is going to share you with anyone else," Jenni said. "I'd want you all to myself."

Marsha giggled.

"He's got a great cock," she said. "It's so big we could both suck on it at the same time."

Jenni froze. This was it. The real moment of truth. Once she got on the bed with both of them, she was agreeing to be their fuck toy. She wondered why the humiliation of the situation was such a fucking turn on. What did it say about her?

"Then let's do it," Jenni said.

The women crawled on the bed and pushed Keith's apart. They lay on their stomachs so that they faced his big black cock. Keith put his hands behind his back. He had a big shit eating grin on his face.

Marsha put the mushroom head of his cock into her mouth while Jenni licked the shaft. Keith closed his eyes and moaned. Marsha switched to licking his shaft while Jenni sucked on his balls. Keith grabbed handfuls of bedsheet and groaned. Marsha stroked his cock while Jenni snaked her hand between Marsha's legs.

Jenni gently explored Marsha's pussy lips before dipping a finger inside her. Marsha moaned. She was wet and hot inside. Jenni found her clitoris and massaged it. Marsha put Keith's cock back in her mouth and moaned again.

Keith put Marsha on her back and put his giant cock inside her. It slid in easily. Seeing Marsha have sex with another man gave Jenni had a moment of jealousy. She swallowed her pride and sucked on Marsha's nipples. Keith grabbed her ankles and pulled her legs further apart.

"Don't stop!" Marsha said. "Either of you. I'm really close."

Jenni nibbled on Marsha's sensitive nipples while Keith rocked his hips and bounced her ass. Marsha rolled her head from side to side as her moans grew louder. Then, she arched her back as her orgasm ripped through her.

Marsha pushed Jenni onto her back and laid on top of her. She alternated between kissing her lips and kissing her breast as she ground her sopping wet pussy against Jenni's pussy. Keith got behind Marsha and entered her again. As he pounded into her from behind, Jenni could feel his balls slapping against her pussy. She looked into Marsha's eyes as another orgasm rippled through her.

Keith pulled out of Marsha and she rolled off of Jenni. Keith got between Jenni's legs and pressed the head of his cock against her pussy lips. Jenni had dreamed of this moment for so long but didn't want not to show how desperately she wanted his cock inside her.

Marsha wrapped her arms around Keith.

"Wait," she said. "I want to taste her first. I've never tasted a woman."

Jenni could see the frustration in Keith's face. It must have matched the frustration in hers. With great self-control, he pulled away.

"Sure, baby," he said. "Have your first taste of pussy."

Marsha looked down at Jenni.

"Can we do this as a sixty-nine?" she said.

"I'd like that," Jenni said.

Marsha straddled Jenni so that her pussy was in Jenni's face. As she lowered herself down, Jenni could feel Marsha's tongue teasing her pussy lips. Jenni licked Marsha's pussy lips and savored the combination of Marsha and Keith's combined musk.

They started slowly, teasing and circling each other's pussy. Marsha didn't eat pussy like a first timer. She slid her fingers inside Jenni as she nibbled her clitoris. She found Jenni's G-spot and massaged it. Johnny never found Marsha's G-spot, but having a pussy helped Jenni find it right away. The two women pushed each other closer and closer to orgasm.

Jenni could feel it starting in her stomach and then spread throughout her body. She mewed like a happy kitten as Marsha's tongue and fingers teased her pussy. Marsha moaned as she licked and prodded. Jenni came first, her legs trembling as her shouts echoed off the walls.

Marsha grabbed Jenni's ass as she ground her pussy into Jenni's mouth. Her hard nipples scraped against Jenni's stomach as Jenni's tongue coaxed her third orgasm out of her.

Marsha rolled off Jenni and wiped Jenni's pussy juice off her mouth with her forearm.

Keith didn't give Jenni time to recover before he got on top of her and slammed his large cock deep inside her wet pussy. Jenni gasped and then sighed with relief. Finally. It was as good as she remembered. She wrapped her arms and legs around him. He grabbed her ass and pounded her.

He left no room for Marsha to join them. He held onto Jenni tightly as he fucked her. Jenni groaned and scratched his back. The bed shook from his violent thrusts. Jenni screamed as her second orgasm exploded inside her. Her flowing pussy juices soaked the bedsheet. She was completely at his mercy.

Suddenly, Keith froze and then his massive cock twitched as his sperm gushed into Jenni's pussy. He grabbed her head and kissed her hard on the lips as he continued to come. Her pussy clutched his cock and milked every last drop out of him.

Sweaty and sated, Keith climbed off of Jenni and sat on the edge of the bed. Marsha stood in front of him with her arms crossed under her breasts.

"You've never fucked me like that," she said. "Should I be jealous?"

Keith laughed nervously.

"I fuck you a lot harder than that," he said. "And no. You have nothing to be jealous about. I have two hot chicks at the same time. Like I'm not going to hit that as hard as I can?"

Jenni was amazed at how well he lied. If Johnny had learned that well to Marsha, they might still be married.

"I could use another drink," Jenni said.

Marsha smiled at Jenni.

"That's a great idea," Marsha said.

"I'll go get us a refill," Keith said.

Jenni watched his tight black buns as he scurried out of the room. She sat with her back against the headboard. Marsha sat next to her. Marsha held Jenni's hand.

"You had your first time with a woman," Jenni said. "Hope I didn't taste too awful."

Marsha put her arm around Jenni's shoulder and had Jenni put her head against her breast.

"I loved how you tasted," Marsha said. "I loved touching another woman's body. I loved touching your body."

Jenni ran her hand on Marsha's leg.

"I loved touching your body too," Jenni said.

"You're just saying that because I paid you for sex," Marsha said.

Jenni pulled away and turned onto her side so that she faced Marsha. She pushed a strand of Marsha's red hair behind her ear.

"It's true that part of my job is complimenting clients," she said. "And sometimes I have to lie. Correction. Often, I have to lie. But then, I find myself with people like you who are too smart to fall for bullshit."

"What do you do with people like me?"

"I either tell the truth or I don't say anything at all." Jenni leaned forward and gently kissed Marsha. "If I didn't love touching you and tasting your sweet pussy and feeling her ass vibrate when you came like a volcano in my mouth, then I wouldn't say it."

Marsha giggled and blushed causing her freckles to stand out.

"Talking like that is making my nipples hard," she said.

"Really? Let me see," Jenni said.

She rubbed Marsha's nipples with her thumb. Marsha sighed happily.

Keith returned with fresh drinks. They lounged on the bed and sipped their drinks. Keith entertained the women by telling them of the worst drunks he's had to deal with working security at the casino.

Keith left to use the bathroom.

"I have to warn you," Marsha said. "Keith has amazing recuperative powers. He's like a teenager. He can fuck two or three times a night."

"You make it sound like it's a bad thing," Jenni said.

"There are times when once is enough for me. But since you're here, I definitely want to fuck again."

The toilet flushed, and Keith returned. Marsha sent him back to wash his hands. When he returned with clean hands, Marsha stroked his cock until it was hard again.

At Keith's suggestion, Jenni got on her hands and knees. Keith got behind her while Marsha lay on her back with her legs spread in front of her. Jenni licked and fingered Marsha while Keith fucked Jenni from behind. The three of them got into a rhythm. Marsha held Jenni's head while Keith held her hips. Jenni was their fuck toy as they worked their way toward coming.

Their moans mingled as their sweaty bodies increased speed. Each became lost in their own erotic pleasure. Jenni loved having Keith fuck her from behind again, even if it did stir up painful memories of the gangbang in the casino basement. Her pussy grew wetter and hotter the longer he pounded into her. She got off on having his strong fingers dig into her and control her. She also loved feeling Marsha's pussy juices flowing into her mouth. She couldn't lap them up fast enough.

"Oh fuck!" Marsha shouted. "I'm going to come. Jenni!"

Jenni was shocked to hear Marsha call her name as she came. She clutched Marsha's ass cheeks as Marsha's body quivered. Behind her, Keith increased his speed as he ground his pelvis against her ass.

"Oh shit!" Keith said. "I can't hold back any longer. Jenni!"

Fuck. Again. Jenni couldn't believe it.

As she felt Keith's huge cock come inside her, an orgasm ripped through her. Her moans were muffled by Marsha's pussy.

Afterwards, Marsha and Jenni took a shower together. They soaped each other's body under the warm water.

Jenni figured that when they paid for her to be there all night that didn't really mean all night. They probably wanted her to get dressed and leave.

To her surprise, they really did want her to stay all night and Jenni found herself under the covers sandwiched between them with Keith's fat flaccid cock nestled against her ass and her arms around Marsha's waist. In many ways sleeping with someone was more intimate than having sex with them. Jenni's heart was beating a mile a minute. She was certain there was no way she could sleep like this. But soon, Keith was snoring into her hair while Marsha slept in her arms.

Jenni's last thought before she drifted off the sleep was that she was glad that Marsha had traded the queen bed for this king. There was no way the three of them could have fit in the queen.

Chapter Eight

It was an hour past dawn when Logan dropped Jenni off at the Moonbeam Motor Lodge. She entered room thirteen and was greeted by two surprises. The first was that Peter wasn't there to collect the money she'd earned during the night. The second was that her room hadn't been cleaned.

Obviously, Brittany didn't clean the room because she was pissed at Jenni. She had every right to be angry. Jenni shouldn't have lectured Brittany on how to live her life. Maybe Mr. Jones didn't care if Brittany gambled. Jenni had been in Vegas long enough to know that most threats were bluffs.

She placed a roll of money, her earnings for the night, on the table in case Peter came by to collect it and left her room. She walked past the pool to room thirty-nine. She knocked on the door. Nobody answered. She knocked again. Still, nobody answered.

She banged on the door with her fist. No answer.

"Damn it, Brittany," Jenni shouted. "Open the fucking door."

Brittany didn't open the fucking door. Jenni gave the door a swift kick and then headed back to her room. She stopped by the pool. She took off her high heels, sat by the edge of the pool, and dipped her feet into the cool water.

She should go for a swim. Swimming helped clear her mind. Maybe later. Right now, she really wanted to talk to Brittany. She wanted to apologize to her best friend. She wanted to tell Brittany about going to Marsha's house. She felt so many conflicting emotions about her evening with Marsha and Keith. She couldn't figure out how she felt about it. In some ways it was the worst thing that ever happened to her. But it had also been an incredible experience.

Brian/Brittany acted like an asshole but deep down she was a good person and a loyal friend. Brittany was the only one of the gamblers turned into escorts with nanobots that had ever met Marsha back when Jenni was Johnny and Brittany was Brian. Brittany was the only person who could fully understand what Jenni was going through.

Jenni considered banging on Brittany's door again, but she was too exhausted. It had been a long strange night and she hadn't slept well. She didn't swim. She went straight to bed.

Chapter 9

Jenni waited outside of room thirteen and watched the last rays of the sun sparkle on the Luxor's dark pyramid. Whenever Jenni watched the sun go down behind it, she felt like she was watching the rise of a dark evil empire. But it was just another flashy hotel in the country's flashiest town.

Logan pulled up in the casino's black town car and Jenni climbed into the back seat. As he pulled out of the parking lot, he glanced at her in the rear-view mirror.

"I'm impressed," he said.

Jenni glanced down at her chest. She wasn't wearing a low-cut dress. Her boobs weren't showing.

"By what?" Jenni said.

"How you're developing a client base," Logan said. "You've done it a lot quicker than most of the other women."

"The client you're taking me to. Did he request me by name?"

"Sure did."

"In Summerlin?"

"Not this time. We're headed downtown."

Jenni leaned back into the cool leather upholstery and looked out the window at the rush hour traffic.

"Peter didn't come by to collect my money," Jenni said. "If you talk to him, let him know that I left it on the table in my room."

Logan drifted into the lane next to him. A car honked, and he quickly veered back into his own lane.

"He was busy last night," Logan said. "That's why he didn't come by. I'm sure he'll be there tomorrow, and you can give him the money for two nights work."

"Whatever," Jenni said.

By the time they reached their destination, the sun had gone down, but the day's heat hadn't left for the night yet. Logan parked in the parking lot of a downtown apartment building. He gave Jenni a room number. She got out of the car and Logan headed back to the motel to pick the next escort to take her to her destination.

Jenni peered up at the beige apartment building. Johnny had lived in one like it. Briefly. During his spiral down from top moneymaker to drowning in debt, he had been able to afford a place like this for a year before he had to move out. They were slightly better than a cheap motel. The apartments were bland and they all had balconies that faced other bland buildings.

Jenni climbed the stairs to the second floor. She found the room number Logan had given her. She wondered who the hell lived here that would ask for her by name. As far as she knew she didn't know anyone who lived in these apartments.

She had a sudden thought. Maybe it was Keith. He didn't live with Marsha. Maybe this was where he lived. Maybe he wanted to see her alone. If this was Keith's apartment, then Jenni was going to give that asshole a piece of her mind. Where the hell did he get off making her do a three way with her ex-wife? Why the fucking dick move? What the hell did Johnny ever do to Keith to deserve that kind of crap?

She was going to tell Keith all that. And then she was going to fuck his brains out because one thing she learned the night before was that she was still addicted to his big black cock.

Jenni pounded on the door. The door opened immediately, and Jenni gasped. It wasn't Keith.

It was Viktor Orlov.

"I can tell from your expression that you are happy to see me," Viktor said.

"I don't get it," Jenni said. "Last time you had me come to a deluxe room in Circus Circus. And now here. Is this your home?"

Viktor stepped out and closed the door behind him.

"Yes," he said. "It is my home. I got room at Circus Circus because I wanted our first time to be special. But now that I've popped your ass cherry there's no need to be special."

"Unless you want to fuck me out here," Jenni said, gesturing at the narrow walkway. "Shouldn't we go inside your apartment?"

Viktor put his arm around Jenni's shoulder.

"Not tonight," he said. "I want to go for ride with you. It's nice night. What do you say?"

"You're paying," Jenni said. "We can do whatever the fuck you want. Speaking of paying."

Jenni held out her palm.

Viktor reached into his pocket and pulled out a wad of bills. He handed them to Jenni. She counted five hundred dollars. That would pay for a car ride. She put the money in her purse and followed Viktor down the stairs to the parking lot.

Viktor wore a black velour track suit that reminded Jenni of Brittany's burgundy velour track suit. She understood that they were comfortable, but she thought they were tacky no matter who wore them. Viktor's gaudy purple tennis shoes made him look extra tacky.

Jenni expected Viktor to also drive a tacky car, but he proved her wrong. He pulled out the key and unlocked a black shiny Lincoln town car. It was identical to the one Logan used to drive the escorts to their clients. In fact, Jenni thought for a moment it was Logan's car and almost got in the back seat.

"You like my car?" Viktor said.

"I ride in one like it every day," Jenni said.

"Yes. Mr. Jones buy these cars for all his men. He likes this car, so I like this car."

They got in the front seat and Viktor turned on the engine. He had left the stereo on and 80s Euro-disco music blared out of the speakers. To Jenni's relief, he turned it down so that it was just a whisper. The steady beat felt like it was the car's heartbeat.

Viktor steered the car out of the parking lot and onto the busy road. After a few blocks, he pulled onto Interstate 515.

"We're alone so you can be honest," Viktor said. "You have been dreaming of my cock. All you can think about is when will Viktor fuck me in the ass again. I am right? Right?"

"You're right," Jenni said. "I've been dreaming of your cock in my ass."

Jenni had been an escort long enough that lying to men about wanting to have sex with them had become second nature. The only thing she remembered about having sex with Viktor was that it was when she had learned to masturbate as a woman and that her ass had been sore for almost a week. She really didn't look forward to him wrecking her ass again.

"Sorry to disappoint you," Viktor said. "But I won't be fucking your ass tonight. Maybe next time."

Jenni breathed a sigh of relief.

Viktor wound through the interchange known as the Spaghetti Bowl and got on Interstate 15. Soon they were leaving Las Vegas. Jenni wondered where the hell he was taking her. There wasn't shit out here but cactus and scorpions.

This was annoying. Not knowing where they were going was annoying. The music was annoying. The beat sounded like someone kicking a drum instead of playing it. Viktor's cologne was annoying. Viktor was annoying. Jenni was thankful that he'd only paid for an hour, but that hour seemed to be taking forever.

"You may be wondering where we are going," Viktor said.

"It had crossed my mind," Jenni said.

"We are going nowhere."

"What?"

"Just for drive."

"Just for a drive? That's it?"

"Not quite. Can you believe I have never gotten blow job while driving?"

Jenni faced the window when she rolled her eyes, so he wouldn't see her do it.

"That is hard to believe, Viktor."

"It is on my bucket list."

"Really?"

"This is perfect place. Not much traffic. Wide open road. Perfect place for me to get blow job while driving."

At least now she knew what was expected of her. Jenni put her hand on Viktor's leg. Viktor spread his legs wider. Jenni reached between his legs and felt around for his cock. She found it and rubbed it through the soft velour material. Viktor took a deep breath and sighed.

"Your hand feels nice," he said. "Your mouth will feel even nicer."

Jenni twisted around in her seat. She reached inside Viktor's pants and pulled out his cock. He wasn't completely hard, but he was getting there. Jenni leaned down and licked the head. Viktor moaned and pushed down on the pedal. The motor roared. Jenni put the head in her mouth and stroked the shaft. Viktor kept one hand on the wheel and put his other hand on top of her head. He pushed her down on his cock. She felt it nudge the back of her throat. She played with his balls while her mouth slid up and down his cock. Viktor pressed down even harder on the pedal and the car sped up.

For the next fifteen minutes, Jenni sucked Viktor's cock while he raced down the highway. He weaved around cars as he gripped the wheel. Jenni didn't know how much longer she could keep sucking when she felt his cock get incredibly hot. She could feel the veins pulsing as Viktor released a steady of come into her mouth. Jenni choked as she tried to swallow it all and some dribbled down his balls

When he was done coming, Jenni licked him clean. She sat back in her seat, opened her purse, and took out a Tic Tac. She popped the breath mint in her mouth and used a tissue to wipe her lips and chin.

Viktor slowed down and pulled onto a dirt road. The car bounced as he drove toward the mountains. The headlights only revealed more dirt road ahead of them.

"Where the fuck are we going, Viktor?" Jenni asked.

"I need to piss," Viktor said.

He pulled around a hill of large boulders and parked the car. He turned off the engine but left the lights on. He got out and stood in front of a pile of rocks with the headlights on his back. Jenni stayed in the car. As he pissed on the rocks, his urine splashed and dribbled down into the sand. When he was done, he shook his cock and put it back in his pants. He faced the car and waved his hand.

"Come, Jenni," Viktor said. "I want to show you something."

Reluctantly, Jenni got out of the car. She started to walk toward Viktor, but he held up his hand.

"Watch out," he said. He pointed at an opening in the rocks. "See. It's a pit. It goes down for miles."

Jenni peered down the pit and then narrowed her eyes at Viktor.

"You've been here before," she said. "Otherwise, how would you have known about that pit?"

Viktor grinned.

"You're right," he said. "I have been here many times. This pit has been very useful for me. It's where I get rid of my problems. Are you a problem, Jenni?"

Icy fingers trickled down Jenni's spine. She looked around. She could try to run but she didn't like her chances of getting away.

"Is that why you brought me out here?" she said. "To get rid of me?"

Viktor laughed. He got in the car. Jenni thought he might leave her out here and she'd have to hitchhike back to town. Instead, he opened the glove compartment and took out a handgun. He slipped it into the waistband of his sweatpants.

"No. I'm just fucking with you. You are not problem. Not yet." Viktor walked around to the back of the car. He popped open the trunk. "Here is my problem."

Shivering, Jenni came around and looked into the trunk. She covered her mouth to keep from screaming. Not that it would have mattered. No one could hear her out here.

Brittany was in the trunk. Her hands were tied behind her and her mouth was gagged. The banging that Jenni had heard was not Viktor's music, but Brittany kicking at the side of trunk.

She had been beaten badly. Her left eye was swollen shut and there was matted blood on her face and in her hair. There were blood stains on her velour jumpsuit.

Viktor grabbed her legs and dragged her out of the trunk. Unable to break her fall, she landed on her back and her head bounced on the hard rocks. She moaned through her gag. Viktor pulled her to her knees. Brittany stared at the ground.

Jenni knelt next to her friend and put her arm around her shoulder.

"What have you done to her?" Jenni said.

Viktor sat on the edge of the open trunk.

"She broke the rules," Viktor said. "She admitted it. The gambling. Fucking for free. Not at first. We had to persuade her to tell the truth. It only took few hours in basement with lead pipe."

Jenni removed the gag. Brittany spat a wad of blood on the ground. Jenni could see that Brittany was missing most of her teeth.

"Please, I'm begging you," Brittany sobbed. A combination of snot and blood poured out of her nose. "Don't kill me. Just let me go. You'll never see me again."

Jenni peered up at Viktor.

"Yes," Jenni said. "Let her go. No one will know you didn't kill her. She'll disappear, and you'll never hear from her again."

Brittany nodded her head as Jenni held her trembling body. Viktor smirked. He grabbed Jenni's arm and yanked her away from Brittany. He then put his hand under Brittany's arm and pulled her to her feet. He put the muzzle of the gun against the side of her head.

"Walk," Viktor said.

Brittany shuffled toward the pit with Viktor behind her. Jenni scrambled to her feet and tried to grab Viktor's arm. He pushed her away. She tumbled to the ground, scraping her hands on the sharp rocks. She got back to her feet and followed them.

"Stop," Viktor said.

Brittany stood at the edge of the pit. She blubbered, too scared to form coherent words.

"You can't do this," Jenni said. "She was just trying to pay off her debt."

Viktor swung his arm around and pointed the gun at Jenni's head. Though she was consumed with fear, Jenni didn't flinch. She stared at Viktor, daring him to pull the trigger.

"You knew she was gambling," Viktor said. "You knew she was breaking the rules. But you said nothing."

"Are you going to kill me too?" Jenni said.

Viktor turned the gun back toward Brittany. He pulled the trigger and the sharp crack echoed off the boulders. The bullet blew a hole in Brittany's head. She tumbled forward and fell into the pit. If she wasn't dead when the bullet entered her brain, she would surely die when her body hit the ground.

Jenni sank to her knees and puked on the rocks.

Viktor peered down the pit.

"Bye bye, problem," he said. "Getting rid of problems makes me hungry. Want to go get pancakes? My treat."

Jenni wiped her mouth with the back of her hand.

"No," she said. "Not hungry."

Viktor shrugged.

"Oh well. Come. Let's go. I take you home."

Jenni struggled to her feet and shuffled to the car. She slumped into the seat. Viktor got behind the wheel, started the engine, and turned back toward the highway. Jenni took a tissue out to wipe the tears from her eyes and any excess puke from her lips.

She popped a Tic Tac into her mouth. She turned and took one last look at the boulders.

"Goodbye, Brian," she whispered.

Jenni had foolishly believed that there were still a few secrets that the casino didn't know about the gamblers. Brittany's death told her a different story. Jenni had no secrets from the casino. She belonged to the casino and they could do whatever they wanted to her.

The End

GENDER SWAP
GAMBLER 5

Chapter One

The stage floor was covered in dollar bills, a gold lame top, and matching gold lame booty shorts. Jenni crouched down to collect her money and her clothes. She wore spiked heels and nothing else. She'd worked enough shifts at Doublemint Armadillo that she no longer thought twice being nude in front of a crowd of horny men. It was part of the job. She strolled off the stage as the DJ announced the next dancer. The next dancer was a petite blonde with big fake tits. The blonde playfully smacked Jenni's butt as they passed each other and then the blonde began gyrating to the music.

Jenni appreciated the smack on the butt. It was a sign that she had been accepted into the stripper sisterhood. It reminded her of how athletes smacked each other on the butt. She paused behind the curtain to put on her clothes and then clutching the dollar bills in her fist, she went to the dressing room.

In the middle of the dressing room was a long table connected to an equally long mirror. A line of stools faced the table. Make-up kits were scattered about on the table. Behind the table were the lockers where the strippers kept their personal belongings. The bathroom and showers were in an adjacent room. Rolling clothing racks held feather boas and other sundry stripper items. Jenni sat at one of the stools and hunched over as she counted her money.

When she finished counting, she rolled the bills into a large roll. She didn't have a rubber band, so she used a hair tie to bind the bills. There were so many bills, they stretched the tie to its limit. Jenni put the roll in her locker in a bag already bulging with rolls of bills. She had never gotten this much in tips dancing before. Still, the fat rolls of money were just a drop in the bucket to what she owed the casino.

The reason for the increase in tips had to do with the fact that the defense contractors convention was this week. The club was packed with representatives of the military industrial complex. Every table was filled with men in uniform with men in expensive suits. The men in the suits paid for the drinks and the strippers, and the men in uniform let them.

Jenni needed to go out on the floor and hustle for a table dance, but she was too exhausted to move. It wasn't the dancing that wore her out. She hadn't been sleeping well this past week. Not since the night she saw her best friend shot in the head. Jenni kept dreaming of Brittany tumbling into a deep pit. In some of the dreams, Jenni was the one falling endlessly.

Brittany. Born a man. Died a woman. Murdered for breaking a stupid rule. Jenni covered her face with her hands and sobbed. Along with the lack of sleep, she'd also been crying a lot. Her emotions were so raw that the least little thing would make the tears flow.

She felt strong arms encircled her and press her wet face against big warm fleshy breasts. A hand patted her head. Jenni hugged her comforter. She knew without opening her eyes that it was Clarissa.

Clarissa was one of Jenni's fellow gender swap gamblers. She knew the reason for Jenni's tears. Jenni had told all the gender swap gamblers about watching Brittany's execution. They needed to know the deadly consequences for breaking Mr. Jones' rules.

"I'm here for you, sister," Clarissa said. "You don't have to carry this alone."

Clarissa yanked a handful of tissues from a box on the table and handed them to Jenni. Jenni dried her eyes and blew her nose.

"Brian was an asshole," Jenni said. "But he was my best friend. He didn't deserve to be shot like a rabid dog."

"You mean, she didn't deserve it," Clarissa said.

Jenni looked at Clarissa in the mirror.

"Look at us," Jenni said. "We're two women in skimpy outfits. Can we still see the men inside? Do they still exist?"

Clarissa narrowed her eyes and then fixed her lipstick.

"Don't give up hope," she said. "Colin and Johnny are still in there and we're going to get motherfucking cocks back. Now let me get you something for those puffy eyes. You can't go out looking like that."

Chapter Two

With Clarissa's help, Jenni was ready to get back to work. She walked through the club, smiling at the men and making small talk. More than once, an arm whipped around her waist and pulled her into the middle of a group of men. Each time, the men only wanted to cop a feel while complimenting her beauty. She'd had so many hands sneak down to squeeze her ass that she hardly noticed when it happened now. Nobody wanted her to sit at their table because they either already had a dancer sitting with them or they were too cheap to buy a thirsty girl a drink.

Jenni was about to give up and go back stage until it was her turn to dance on stage when a waitress pulled her aside. The waitress' name was Audrey. She could have been a dancer. She had the body for it. But she chose to stick with serving drinks. Somebody had to.

"You got a customer waiting for you in room two," Audrey said.

Jenni's forehead furrowed. Room two was one of the private rooms reserved for customers who wanted a secluded lap dance. They weren't as secluded or as spacious as the V.I.P. lounges. They were dark rooms with barely enough space for the dancer and the customer. Unlike the V.I.P. lounges, there were hidden security cameras in the private rooms. So much for privacy.

"That's weird," Jenni said.

"Yeah," Audrey agreed. "He claims he tried to ask you himself but couldn't get your attention."

"What's his name?"

"The only name he gave me was Andrew Jackson."

Audrey held up a twenty dollar bill.

Jenni shrugged and headed for room two. Usually when a guy wanted a private dance, he asked the dancer and the dancer had a waitress check to see if there was a room available. This was the first time that Jenni knew of when a customer made the arrangement directly with the waitress without checking with the dancer first. Not only was it unusual, it was presumptuous of the customer to assume Jenni would be available.

When Jenni got to room two, she hesitated before going in. She wished she had asked Audrey for a description of the man waiting for her inside the room. She hoped he didn't work for the Pentagon. Those guys got billions of taxpayer money but were notorious in strip clubs for being penny-pinching bastards.

Sometimes the lap dances in the private rooms led to sex, but most times they didn't. Most of the guys who could only afford a private room didn't have enough money left over to tip a dancer enough for her to let him put his cock inside one of her orifices.

Jenni put her hand on the doorknob and froze. An image flashed in her mind that

305

Viktor was inside waiting to put a bullet in her head. She took a step back and clenched her fists. She needed to get a grip on herself. It couldn't be Viktor. If he was going to kill her, it wouldn't be here. Even he wasn't crazy enough to shoot someone in a crowded titty bar.

Jenni took a deep breath and entered room two. It took a minute for her eyes to adjust to the darkness. When she was finally able to see the man sitting on the love seat waiting for her, she resisted the urge to flee the room. It wasn't Viktor. It was someone much worse.

Chapter Three

Keith smiled at Jenni.

"What the fuck are you doing here?" Jenni said.

Keith jumped to his feet.

"I had to tell you," he said. "I had nothing to do with Brittany. I didn't even know it was going to go down like that. I thought Mr. Jones was just going to warn her."

Jenni crossed her arms under her breasts.

"Bullshit," she said. "I know from personal experience that you've helped work people over in the basement."

"I've never hurt anybody. Mr. Jones only has me break in the newly made women," he said. "I thought he was done with busting kneecaps and breaking heads."

"Did you know he still had people killed?"

Keith's eyes widened.

"Killed? No fucking way. Mr. Jones wouldn't kill anybody. All he did was make Brittany leave town."

"Is that what he told you?"

"Not directly."

"Whoever told you that lied. Mr. Jones had Viktor put a bullet in Brittany's head and then had her body dumped into a pit in the desert."

Keith glared at Jenni.

"Now you're the one talking bullshit," he said.

"I was there when it happened," Jenni said. "Viktor made me watch."

Keith sat on the loveseat and stared at the floor.

"That sick son of a bitch," he said. "Bad enough he agreed to kill Brittany, but to drag you along. That guy is fucking crazy."

Jenni leaned against the wall.

"Let's say I believe you," she said. "And I'm not sure that I do. What the fuck was that shit at Marsha's place all about?"

Keith smiled sheepishly.

"Yeah, that was some wild shit, wasn't it?" he said.

Jenni slapped Keith across the face. He was shocked, but he didn't retaliate. He held his face and stared at her.

"What'd you do that for?" Keith said.

"What did Johnny do that makes you hate him so much?" Jenni said.

"I don't hate Johnny. I certainly don't hate you."

"Come on. Johnny must have done something that pissed you off so fucking bad that it drove you to torture me the way you did."

Keith stood again. He held out his hands in a helpless gesture.

"What are you talking about?"

Jenni put her hands on her hips.

"I find out that you're fucking my ex-wife," she said. "And how do I find out? When you have me come to my old house.

And then, you fuck her right in front of me. But that wasn't enough for you. You also fuck me in front of her. Talk about some sick shit."

Keith tried to put his hand on Jenni's shoulder, but she knocked it away.

"It wasn't like that," he said. "I swear. I would have come here to see you, but I only found out you were working here yesterday."

Jenni narrowed her eyes at Keith.

"You were going to bring Marsha here?" she said.

Keith waved his hands.

"No, no, no," he said. "You don't understand. I really wanted to see you."

"See me? What are you talking about?"

Keith shrugged his shoulders.

"I had to see you again. I've broken in every gender swap gambler. It's a weird job. The weirdest I've ever had. But I'm damn good at what I do. And once I'm done, I don't think about the woman again. That is until I broke you in. Once you gave in, you were amazing. You were the hottest piece of ass I've ever had. That goes for women born women and men turned into women. I couldn't stop thinking about you. So, you see? I had to have you again."

Jenni was flabbergasted. She sat on the love seat.

"That is the most fucked up thing anyone has ever said to me," she said. "But that doesn't explain why make me do it with you and Marsha?"

Keith sat next to Jenni. Their knees touched.

"I knew you used to be married to Marsha," Keith said, "but from what Marsha told me that ended a long time ago. I figured you wouldn't care. I really like Marsha. We have a good thing going, but it's not exclusive. She sees other guys and I see other girls. But I didn't want to go behind her back."

"So, you talked her into having a second woman in bed?" Jenni said.

"It wasn't that hard."

"Either you're a liar or an idiot."

"I guess I'm an idiot. I thought we had a great time together."

Jenni couldn't believe what she was hearing. He had the hots for her. It would be stupid to lie and not admit that she wanted his cock as much as he wanted her pussy. He would know she was lying. He had made her addicted to his cock. He knew she couldn't resist it.

Keith wore a plaid shirt and sweatpants. Jenni could see the outline of his huge black cock in the fabric of the sweatpants. She was about to put her hand in his lap when someone knocked on the door. They both jumped. Jenni answered. Audrey poked her head in.

"Would you like to order a drink?" she said.

"Yeah," Jenni said. "Bourbon on the rocks." She turned to Keith. "What about you?"

"Nothing right now," he said.

Jenni glared at him.

"You have to order something," she said. "Besides, you're already buying me a drink."

"Okay. A beer."

Audrey nodded and left.

As soon as the door closed behind her, Keith got to his feet and wrapped her arms around Jenni. She could feel his cock rubbing against her ass. She wiggled out and pushed him back onto the loveseat. She nodded at the ceiling.

"They're watching us," Jenni said. "I'm supposed to be dancing."

Keith raised an eyebrow.

"Good," he said. "I'd like to see you dance."

Jenni held out her hand.

"Pay me first."

Keith dug his wallet out of his pocket.

"Damn," he said. "I forgot how titty bars make you pay for every damn thing."

He handed Jenni money. She counted it and then slipped it into her garter belt.

"This is enough for three dances or one lap dance," she said. "Which one do you want?"

Keith took enough money out of his wallet to pay for another lap dance.

"Let's start with a lap dance," he said. "We'll see how things go from there."

Jenni began to move to the music playing in the club which was loud enough to be heard in the private room. She pushed Keith's legs apart, turned, and bent over until her ass was in his lap. She gyrated against his groin. Shivers ran through her body.

She faced him and smirked at the way his cock pressed against the fabric of his sweatpants.

There was a knock at the door. Audrey had arrived with their drinks. Keith paid her and gave her a tip. He put his bottle aside without taking a sip. Jenni swallowed half of her Bourbon and savored the way it burned her throat.

Jenni began dancing with her back to Keith again. She rotated her hips and bounced her ass. She put her hands on his knees and rubbed her ass up and down on his crotch. She could feel his cock pressed between her ass cheeks. Keith moaned with pleasure.

She turned and leaned toward so he could see down her cleavage. She straddled the love seat and sat in his lap facing him. She dry-humped him. The small room filled with the heady scent of their combined musk. Her mouth watered for the taste of his salty come. Keith grabbed her ass and grinded against her crotch.

Jenni could have fucked him right then and there. Her pussy was aching to feel his huge cock fill her up. It was more than lust. She hoped that getting lost in erotic pleasure would help alleviate the overwhelming sadness of losing Brittany.

But now that Jenni knew that Keith wanted her as much as she wanted him, she was going to use that to her advantage. She was going to tease him as long as possible. He had tortured her by having her come to Marsha's house for a threesome. It was his turn to be tortured.

She pulled off her gold lame top and her breasts bounced free. She pressed them against his face. He sucked on her nipple. Erotic sensations coursed through her. Her pussy tingled with anticipation. She pulled away and kissed him. He dug his tongue into her mouth. She sucked on it like she was eventually going to suck his cock.

She continued to hump him. Her body naked except for the booty shorts. The song ended and Keith quickly shoved the money for another lap dance into her hands. She added the bills to her garter belt.

Jenni drank the rest of her Bourbon. Keith swallowed half of his beer. A new song started and she turned her back to Keith and smacked her butt. Then she rubbed her ass against his cock. It was hard as a rock and practically burning a hole through his sweatpants. She leaned back against his chest. He grabbed her tits and pinched her nipples. She moaned. She reached under her ass and massaged his cock. He moaned. She could taste the sex in the air.

She straddled him again and grinded on his cock. He cried out in frustration. She leaned in so that she was close to his ear.

"Do you want to fuck me?" she said.

"Yes," Keith said. "It's taking every ounce of restraint to keep from creaming my pants."

"You know the rules. No money. No sex."

"I'll pay you anything you want if you'll let me fuck you right now."

"Really?"

"Yes. How much do you want?"

"How much do you have in your wallet?"

Keith almost knocked Jenni out of his lap so that he could get to his wallet. She leaned against the wall as he opened his wallet and took out every bill he had. His hand trembled as he handed her the cash. She counted it up. She didn't care why he had twenty-five hundred dollars in his wallet. She put it all in her garter belt.

She drank the rest of her Bourbon and then shimmied out of her gold lame booty shorts. Her pussy glistened it was so wet with excitement.

"Damn, your pussy smells so fucking good," Keith said.

Jenni got on her knees in front of Keith and pulled his sweatpants down to his ankles. His cock sprang free. So much pre-come had oozed out of the slit it was if he'd already ejaculated. She licked the pre-come off his cock and then licked her lips.

"Yummy," she said.

She grabbed the shaft and put the head in her mouth. Keith leaned back and groaned loudly. She slurped loudly as her mouth went up and down his cock. She massaged his balls as she sucked his cock. Keith ran his hands through her brunette hair.

"Please," he begged. "I don't want to come in your mouth. I need your sweet pussy. I need it now."

Jenni let his cock pop out of her mouth. She smiled wickedly as she straddled him. She guided his cock to her pussy lips. She sighed as she impaled herself on his giant rod.

She rode him hard and fast, her pussy taking his entire length inside her. She put her arms around his neck and smashed her tits in his face. He put his arms around her waist and humped her. Their combined juices soaked the loveseat.

"You teased me for too long," Keith panted. "I can't hold back much longer."

319

"Don't hold back," Jenni said. "Give it to me. I want to feel you come inside me."

Keith dug his fingers into her soft ass flesh as his cock spurted hot semen inside her pussy setting off her own orgasm. She gritted her teeth. Explosions rocked her body. She rotated on his cock as her pussy lips milked his cock.

They held onto to each other as their sexual vibrations subsided.

Finally, Jenni climbed off of Keith. There was a box of tissues in the room for these moments. She wiped as much of his sperm off her pussy and tossed the sticky tissues into a wastebasket. Keith pulled up his sweatpants and downed the last of his beer. Jenni put her gold lame top and shorts back on.

"Don't tell Marsha we did this," Keith said.

Jenni glared at Keith.

"You said you two weren't exclusive. She sees other guys and you see other girls," Jenni said.

"Yeah," Keith said. "But we don't talk about it. It's just understood."

Give me a break, Keith. I was a man, remember? I know how this works. You say it's not exclusive, but Marsha doesn't know that. I don't fucking believe this. You just cheated on my ex-wife with me."

Keith shrugged.

"You should be flattered."

"I'm not. Look, Keith. You're right. My marriage to Marsha ended a long time ago. But that doesn't mean I don't care what happens to her. I'll fuck you anytime you want. But only if she knows about it. Okay?"

"Okay. I'll tell her."

Jenni figured he was lying. It didn't matter. If he didn't tell Marsha, she would.

Chapter Four

Jenni stood with the tourists and watched the Bellagio's fountain show. The rows of water shot into the air in time with Michael Jackson's Billy Jean. Jenni had seen the fountains dozens of times set to dozens of songs, but she the patterns of the cascading water still mesmerized her. She enjoyed the feel of the spray washing over her.

She glanced at her wristwatch. She had to hurry to see her next client. Her red boots clopped on the concrete sidewalk as she approached the hotel. Working long hours as both a stripper and an escort had left her with aching muscles and sleepy. She wondered who she had to fuck to get a good night's sleep.

She took the elevator to the eighth floor and knocked on her client's door. A tall handsome black man answered. He smiled showing perfect teeth.

"You must be Jenni," he said in a deep baritone.

Jenni was suddenly wide awake. She no longer felt embarrassed when she was attracted to a man. This guy was wearing a skin-tight T-shirt that showed off his muscular body and a pair of tight jeans that showed off his impressive package. Jenni's knees weakened at the thought of peeling off those jeans.

"That's me," Jenni said. "May I come in?"

"Of course, please come in."

He held the door open for her. Jenni entered. She looked around. It was not one of the hotel's best rooms, but still a good room. Though he was wearing worn out tennis shoes, two pairs of brightly polished black dress shoes were lined up in front of the bed. An army dress uniform hung on the closet door. Jenni had been with a wide variety of men, but never a military man.

"I understand the proper protocol is that I pay you first," the soldier said.

He handed Jenni a folded stack of bills. Her eyebrow raised as she counted the money.

"This is enough for the entire evening," Jenni said. "Was that your intention or are you just being generous?"

"Your services are required for the entire evening," he said.

"I'll need to let my driver know that I'll be staying longer than expected."

"Absolutely."

Jenni called Logan and gave him the news. He instructed her to call him when she was ready to be picked up. After she hung up, she put her phone away and smiled at the soldier.

"Shall we go to the bedroom?" she said.

The soldier grimaced.

"Actually," he said. "We need to go now."

Jenni's stomach tied in a knot. The last time a client wanted her to go somewhere, she ended up watching her best friend's execution.

"Go?" Jenni said. "Go where?"

"I'm sorry, but that's classified information."

Jenni walked over to the coffee table and placed the money on top.

"Sorry, mister," she said. "But I don't play that game. You'll have to get another girl."

She headed for the door, but he blocked her from leaving. He held up his hands.

"Please," he said. "Let me explain. I'm sure you know that this week is the defense contractor convention."

Jenni crossed her arms.

"Sure," she said. "And I see from the uniform hanging over there that you're in the army."

"There's a lot of money riding on defense contracts. The reps from these companies will do anything to try and influence the armed forces to choose them. That includes fancy dinners, shows, strip clubs..."

"And escorts."

"Exactly." He smiled and showed his beautiful teeth again. "The defense contractors aren't interested in wining and dining a guy like me because I'm just a grunt. But they've been doing everything they can to get to my commanding officer."

Jenni laughed.

"I get it," she said. "Your commanding officer didn't want one of those reps to get him a call girl. Not only would it not be his choice, but it would look pretty bad. So, he had you do set it up."

"Wow. You'd make a pretty good commanding officer yourself. That's our covert operation. I order you to my room, and then I sneak you over to his room at a different hotel."

Jenni walked back to the coffee table and snatched up the money. She put it in her pink purse.

"Okay," she said. "Let's go see your commanding officer."

He led the way out of the room. As she walked behind him, she admired his firm ass and lamented that he wasn't her client after all.

Chapter Five

Jenni and the soldier rode the elevator down to the parking garage. They got into his rental car, an unassuming blue Captiva. Jenni worried about how far they would have to travel for this secret mission, but it turned out they only traveled six miles to the Four Queens Hotel.

Jenni shivered when she saw the sign for the Four Queens. Johnny's last hand of poker was four queens. He lost his gender on four queens.

The soldier told Jenni which room to go to and dropped her off at the hotel lobby. As soon as she shut the car door, he drove off. Jenni was surprised that a high-ranking officer in the armed forces was staying here. It was an old hotel in need of renovation. Then again, not many defense contractors would be hanging around Glitter Gulch.

Jenni went to the room the soldier had told her to go to and knocked on the door. A man slightly taller than her answered the door. He was in his late forties. He had a high and tight regulation haircut. What little hair was on the top of his head was black with specks of gray. His Polo shirt and gray slacks clung to his body and revealed that was in incredible shape. He looked Jenni up and down like he was inspecting his troops. Jenni decided to play along.

"Jenni Jones reporting for duty," Jenni said.

A big smile spread across his face.

"Come aboard, soldier," he said.

Jenni entered the room and looked around. It was one of the hotel's regal suites. This was the hotel's best room, though it was small and stodgy compared to the glitzy opulence of the strip hotel suites. Personally, she loved rooms like this with their brown leather chairs and blonde wood cabinets. It even smelled old-fashioned and reminded her of Las Vegas' bad old days of the mob, Elvis, and Sinatra.

"Holt Cooper," he said.

He squeezed Jenni's hand with too much force. She grimaced. He realized his mistake and loosened his grip. Jenni tried not to look like she was snooping as she gazed at his room. He didn't leave his military clothes where she could see them, but she figured he was probably his ranking was pretty high if he was able to have a soldier deliver an escort as if she were a pizza.

"Now that I'm here," Jenni said. "I'm curious to find out how you plan to conquer me. What's your battle plan?"

Holt put his hands on his hips, threw back his head, and laughed.

"No battle plan necessary," he said. "Were on the same side. But rather than just jump in the sack, I'd like to play a few hands of poker."

Jenni's mouth went dry.

"Poker?" she said. "I can't. I don't gamble. It's against my religion."

Holt cocked his head to the side.

"Really?" he said. "And you live here in the gambling capital of the world."

Jenni was torn. Her life depended on following the three rules, but she was also supposed to do whatever she could to please a client.

"Well, I used to play. But I had to stop. I had a gambling problem."

Holt grinned.

"Don't worry," he said. "We're not playing for money. This is strip poker. It makes taking your clothes off more fun for me."

Jenni thought about it. There would be no money involved so it wasn't really gambling. There wasn't much difference between this and playing for Tic Tacs with the other gender swap gambler. Jenni always considered strip poker a silly game but if her

331

client got off on playing silly games, then that was what they would do.

"Okay," Jenni said. "Let's play."

"Good," Holt said. "I can't wait to start making you lose your clothes."

"How do you know you won't lose your clothes to me?"

"Either way I win."

Holt only had Gin and tonic so he made two Gin and tonics. He put a fresh pack of cards on a round table. On one side of the table was a sitting area and on the other side was the bed. Jenni could feel the familiar ache in her fingers to get cards in her hands. She flexed them in anticipation. After Holt removed the cards from the cardboard holder, she noticed that he flexed his fingers as well. That told her that he was as addicted to gambling as she was.

Jenni purposely folded early on the first few hands to see what kind of player Holt was. He had skill and probably won consistently with most the people he played, but he wouldn't stand a chance with a professional gambler. He had too many tells and he didn't bluff as well he thought he did.

The gambler in Jenni wanted to take him down. Strip him naked and show him how a real gambler played. But then, it was also fun to control the game and manipulate him into believing that he was the better player

Each time she lost, Jenni made a show out of removing an item of clothing. She unzipped and removed her boots slowly and made sure he got a clear view of her legs. She teased him by reaching for the back of her dress, but then removing her earrings instead. Holt didn't seem to mind. He wanted Jenni, but he also wanted to play cards.

Jenni won until she had Holt down to his T-shirt and boxer shorts. She giggled at her good luck and licked her lips at his body. This he did seem to mind. He was not a good loser and he glared at her every time she had a winning hand.

Jenni caught the warning. She didn't want to piss off her client. It was bad for business and more importantly, nobody knew where she was. Maybe he was the kind of guy who hurt women when his pride was wounded and maybe he wasn't. Jenni didn't plan to find out.

When she could, she purposely lost, but if she got a really good hand, she folded early. Soon, she was down to her bra and panties. They were both see-through, so she was practically naked.

She tried to lose the next hand, she really did, but Holt was so distracted by her body that he kept lost. He stripped off his T-shirt, revealing a well-developed chest and rock-hard abs. He wasn't a big man, but he was compact and solid muscle. But Jenni didn't take the time to admire his body. She saw how his face was getting red.

Rather than chance him losing again, Jenni folded on the next hand even though she had three aces and two Jacks. She reached back and unhooked her bra, but then she wrapped her arm over her bra to keep it in place. She lowered the left strap and then the right. Holt watched her every move. Finally, she let the bra drop, revealing her breasts. Her pink nipples reacted to the cool air conditioning. She squeezed her breasts and pushed them together before letting them bounce.

"Are those real?" Holt said.

"You'll find out soon enough," Jenni said.

She wondered if his erection was making a tent in his boxer shorts, but she would have had to look under the table to find out.

Holt dealt the next hand. He picked up his cards and changed their order. He looked over at Jenni. Her cards were still on the table. She hadn't touched them.

"Come on," he said. "This could be the last hand."

Jenni thrust out her chest. Her nipples ached for attention. She lowered her eyes into slits. She put her palm on the cards.

"I fold," she said.

Holt's eyes widened.

"How can you fold?" he said. "You don't know what's in your hand."

"I don't want cards in my hand. I want your cock in my hand. And in my mouth. And in my pussy. Please don't make me wait any longer."

Holt slapped his cards on the table and stood. Sure enough, his erection was making a tent in his boxer shorts. Jenni stood as well. He came to her side of the table and swooped her up into his arms. Jenni had never been in anyone's arms before. It was more fun than she thought it would be.

Holt carried her to the bed. He lay her on her back and yanked off her panties. He pulled her legs apart and planted his mouth on her pussy. He lapped away with great enthusiasm, but the truth was his shock and awe technique caused Jenni more pain than pleasure.

"Please," she fake-moaned. "I want your cock so fucking bad. Please bring it up here."

Jenni was relieved that he was willing to follow orders. Holt scrambled off the bed and stripped off his boxer shorts. His erection bobbed. He was at least eight inches. Though Jenni melted into a puddle when Keith rammed his twelve-inch monster into her, eight inches was her favorite size cock.

Jenni sat up with her back against the headboard. Holt stood on the bed with his feet on either side of her. His cock bobbed in her face. She put him deep into her mouth to get him wet. Once he was slick with spit, she stroked his shaft while sucking the head.

"That's good," Holt said. "Suck that dick. Suck it good."

Jenni stifled a laugh. Even during sex, he liked to give orders.

She swallowed him down to the base and pressed her nose into his pubic hair. The musky smell and taste of his cock was making her pussy wet. She gently massaged his balls and then snaked a finger to the base of his asshole. He bucked his hips so that his cock banged against the back of her throat. He held her head still and face fucked her, ramming his cock in and out of her mouth. She opened her mouth wide while drool dripped off her chin.

Holt let go of her head and pulled his cock out of her mouth. Jenni gasped for breath.

"I want to tit fuck you," he said.

Jenni answered by holding her breasts up. He pinched her nipples until she gasped in pain and then he slid his cock between her tits. She pressed her breasts together to make a nice warm sleeve for him. Holt held onto the headboard as he fucked her tits. Each time the head of his cock popped up between her breasts, Jenni licked it.

He pulled away and climbed off the bed. He motioned for her to join him on the floor. Jenni wasn't sure what he wanted to do. But then he picked her up as if she weighed nothing and impaled her on his cock. She yelped as he buried his cock all the way inside her pussy.

It was an amazing sensation. He had total control of her body. Her legs stuck out on either side of his torso as he slid her up and down on his cock. His strong hands gripped her ass and pulled her more open to his assault. She held onto his shoulders. She was his fuck toy. She shut her eyes and rode the sensations bubbling through her.

There was a warm feeling in her stomach as she got closer and closer to an orgasm. But just as she was at the moment of release, he pulled her off his cock and placed her on the bed. He had her get on her hands and knees at the edge of the bed, so he could stand behind her and enter her from that position.

Jenni gripped the bedsheets and Holt grabbed her hips as he fucked her from behind. Soon, that familiar warmth returned, and Jenni inched toward the orgasm she had been denied. But then, Holt pulled his cock out of her dripping pussy again.

For the rest of the night, Holt fucked Jenni in a variety of positions. He was on top of her and then had her straddle him. He followed that by having her do a reverse Cowgirl. And then he plucked her off the bed and placed her on the table and fucked her on top of the table. And then he did another position. Each time, he would drive Jenni to the brink of orgasm and then pull out.

Jenni was glad she swam laps every day or else she wouldn't have had the physical stamina to keep up with Holt. They fucked all night. As the first rays of sunrise began to bleed through the blinds, they were drenched with sweat and Jenni was whimpering from being on the edge of orgasm.

They were on the bed in the Missionary position. Holt was pounding her pussy and driving her closer to the orgasm she desperately needed. If she didn't come soon she was going to lose her mind. But just as she was about to come, he pulled out of her. He straddled her sweaty body and jerked his cock until he spurted reams of sticky cum on her tits.

Holt fell back and laughed as he wiped sweat off his face.

"Damn," he said. "I needed that."

Jenni wanted to cry. Every fiber of her being was tingling with need. She swallowed her frustration and pasted a smile on her face.

"That was a man who needed to come," she said.

"You were fucking amazing," Holt said.

He climbed off the bed and threw open the curtains. The morning sun streamed in. He took a deep breath and then dropped to the floor and began to do push-ups.

Jenni looked down at her body. She was covered in sweat and sperm. She stank of sex.

"Do you mind if I take a shower?" she said.

"Be my guest," Holt said as he continued to do push-ups.

On wobbly legs, Jenni went into the bathroom. She got into the shower and made the water as hot as she could stand it. Washing sweat off after strenuous exercise always made her feel clean and fresh.

After soaping her body, she stood under the shower, letting the hot water sooth her aching muscles. She was still frustrated over the lack of orgasm. She didn't expect a client to make her come. In fact, most didn't. But Holt had gotten her so fucking close.

Jenni rubbed the outer lips of her pussy. She used on hand to hold her lips open and with her other hand, she used her fingers to tease her clitoris. She sighed as heat emanated through her body. Her nipples stiffened. She reached deeper and rubbed her G-spot. She closed her eyes as she felt the warmth in her stomach spreading.

She concentrated on her clitoris, jerking it like a little cock. Every muscle in her body tensed as she inched closer. She gritted her teeth and rubbed faster. Finally, it arrived. The full released of the long-awaited orgasm exploded inside her. She cried out and her body quivered as wave after wave pulsed through her.

But that was just the beginning. Her body was too ready for coming. She masturbated until she came three more times. She was exhausted by the time she climbed out of the shower. She toweled her body dry.

Jenni left the bathroom with a towel wrapped around her body. Holt had made two cups of coffee. Hotel room coffee sucked, but Jenni welcomed the caffeine. They sat at the same table that they had played cards on and fucked on.

"Sorry I took so long," Jenni said. "In the shower."

"Not a problem," Holt said. He took a sip of his coffee. "As you probably noticed, I'm a fitness freak. It's a thing with military folks. Most escorts can't keep up with me, but you passed the endurance test."

"You did most of the work. I just had to lie there for most of it."

Holt reached across the table and patted Jenni's hand.

"No need to be modest. You're a tough lady. And you deserve a tip for being all you can be."

Holt went to the bed and got a set of keys off the nightstand. He opened the closet. Inside was the safe that hotels provide guests in their rooms. Holt unlocked the safe and swung the door open. He had his back to her so Jenni couldn't see inside. But then he turned around. He had an envelope in his hand. The envelope was filled with money. As Holt selected some bills from the envelope, Jenni had full view of the inside of the safe. It held a metal briefcase. Jenni had no idea why but something about that briefcase gave her goosebumps.

Holt put the envelope back in the safe and relocked it. He closed the closet and handed Jenni the bills. She didn't count it. She would do that later. She thanked Holt with a kiss.

While Jenni got dressed, Holt called his soldier to come pick Jenni up. She met the soldier in the hotel lobby. He drove her back to the Bellagio and dropped her off by the fountain.

Jenni waited until Logan had picked her up and they were headed back to the Moonbeam Motor Lodge before she checked to see how much Holt had tipped her. It was the same amount he had paid for her to spend the evening with him. She had made double that night. If every client paid this much, she'd be able to pay off her debt to the casino in a couple of months.

Chapter Six

The following night, Logan took Jenni back to Summerlin.

"This neighborhood loves you," Logan said.

"Apparently," Jenni said.

When Logan parked in front of Marsha's house, Jenni didn't panic like last time. She knew what to expect now and couldn't help but smile. She might be a real sick puppy, but she had a great time having sex with Marsha and Keith and was thrilled that they wanted her to do it again. She was giddy as she rang the doorbell.

Marsha answered. Her broad smile was contagious. Jenni smiled back at her.

"I'm so glad to see you again," Marsha said.

"Me too," Jenni said.

They hugged. Jenni breathed in Marsha's perfume. She followed Marsha into the house. Marsha led the way to the living room.

"Have a seat," Marsha said. "I just opened a bottle of white wine. Would you like some?"

"I would love a glass," Jenni said.

Actually, Jenni never cared for white wine, but she didn't feel like getting hammered so white wine was perfect.

Marsha went into the kitchen. Jenni glanced around the room and wondered when Keith was going to show himself. Marsha returned with two glasses of wine. She handed one to Jenni and put hers on the coffee table. She sat next to Jenni on the couch.

Marsha tapped her fingers on her knee. Jenni knew her ex-wife well enough to know that meant Marsha had something difficult to say and wasn't sure how to begin.

"Is everything okay?" Jenni said.

Marsha sighed.

"Keith won't be joining us tonight," she said. "I hope that's okay."

Jenni wasn't sure if that was okay or not. She had looked forward to both Keith's big black cock and Marsha's sweet pussy. Just getting one of the two was still a treat for her.

"That's fine," Jenni said. "I get you all to myself. Is everything okay between you and Keith?"

"I don't know," Marsha said. "I feel like he's been keeping secrets from me. My ex-husband used to keep secrets and I swore I wouldn't put up with that again."

That stung. Jenni felt like Marsha had plunged a knife into her chest. What made it worse was that Marsha was right. Johnny had been a lousy husband. He had kept secrets from Marsha when he should have been honest with her.

Jenni took Marsha's hand.

"I'm sorry to hear that," Jenni said.

"It's my fault," Marsha said. "I don't want a serious relationship. He's free to see other people. I just want him to tell me."

"Are you sure he's seeing someone else?"

"I don't have proof, but I can just tell."

Jenni chewed on her lower lip. How could she tell Marsha that the someone else Keith was seeing was her? Jenni had planned to tell Marsha about her and Keith if Keith didn't tell Marsha himself, but now she couldn't bring herself to do it.

Jenni glanced down at her slutty clothes and her heart sank. She had to be honest. She was just the prostitute that Keith and Marsha hired for sex. She had no right to get involved in their relationship.

"I'm sorry, Marsha," Jenni said. "Keith seemed like a nice guy."

Marsha sipped her wine.

"He's a good guy," Marsha said. "But he's not very bright. He lies because he's too stupid to tell the truth."

Jenni laughed which made Marsha laugh.

"I didn't tell Keith that I was having you come here tonight," Marsha said. "Maybe I'm not bright enough to tell the truth."

Jenni put her hand on Marsha's knee.

"Or maybe," Jenni said. "Just maybe. It's none of his damn business."

It was if Jenni's words had flipped a switch in Marsha. She lunged for Jenni and threw her arms around her. They kissed and fondled each other like they were on a prom date.

Jenni was equally shocked and impressed when Marsha lowered the zipper on Jenni's dress and pulled it down to her waist. Before Jenni could attempt to unbutton Marsha's blouse, Marsha had unhooked Jenni's bra.

Jenni removed her bra and felt the cool air on her breasts. Marsha warmed them up by sucking on Jenni's nipples. Jenni mewed like a happy kitten. She put her hand between Marsha's legs and squeezed her pussy through

351

her shorts. Then she snaked her hand inside Marsha's shorts and past her panties. Her pussy was hot and wet. Marsha shuddered and playfully bit Jenni's left nipple.

"Why are we on the couch when there's a perfectly good bed down the hall?" Marsha said.

"Good point," Jenni said.

Marsha took Jenni's hand and led her to the bedroom. Before Jenni could take her dress off, Marsha did it for her. She yanked it down and had her step out of it. Marsha stood behind Jenni and slipped her hand inside Jenni's panties. She fingered Jenni's pussy while she pinched her nipple. Jenni leaned back into Marsha. Her ex-wife had taken control of her and she loved it. Her body felt like it was on fire. She rubbed her ass against Marsha as Marsha's fingers opened her up.

Marsha pulled her fingers out and Jenni whimpered at their absence. She turned around and frantically unbuttoned Marsha's blouse. As Jenni unzipped Marsha's shorts, Marsha unhooked her bra and tossed it aside. Jenni pulled Marsha's shorts and panties down to her ankles. She got on her knees in front of Marsha so that Marsha could step out of her shorts. Jenni flung them aside. Seeing she was facing Marsha's pussy, Jenni massaged Marsha's ass as she kissed Marsha's pussy. Marsha spread her legs wider so that Jenni could lick her pussy lips.

Marsha moaned as Jenni teased her clitoris with her tongue. Jenni put her finger inside Marsha. It was like sticking her finger inside a furnace.

"Oh shit," Marsha said. "Keep doing that. Don't change a thing."

Jenni continued licking and fingering Marsha. Marsha shuddered violently as she had her first orgasm. Jenni lapped up her flowing pussy juices as she came into her mouth.

Marsha stepped back and helped Jenni to her feet. They kissed.

"There's something I'd like to do," Marsha said. "You can say no."

Jenni grinned nervously.

"Okay," she said. "What is it?"

"Wait here."

Marsha dashed into the bathroom connected to the bedroom. Jenni was naked except for her panties, so she took them off. She realized she hadn't gotten the money first. She was breaking the first rule, but she didn't care. The rule was no money, no sex. From the way Marsha was making her feel, this was beyond sex. This was lovemaking.

Marsha returned. Jenni stared at Marsha's crotch. She laughed and pointed before she could stop herself. Marsha blushed a deep red and turned back toward the bathroom. Jenni dashed to her and grabbed her arms.

"I'm sorry," Jenni said. "I didn't mean to react that way. It's just this was the last thing I expected. Though now that I see it, I don't know why I didn't suggest it myself."

Marsha smiled shyly and then pushed out her hips proudly.

She wore a strap-on with a nine-inch realistic dildo complete with veins and a mushroom head that was very stiff and erect. Jenni kissed Marsha as she stroked the dildo.

"You like it?" Marsha said.

"I do," Jenni said. "I can't wait to try it out."

They climbed onto the bed. Marsha got on her knees and Jenni lay on her stomach in front of her. Jenni sucked on the dildo. Marsha brushed Jenni's hair aside, so she could see clearly.

"It's almost like having a cock," Marsha said. "Have you ever wondered what it would be like to be a man?"

Jenni choked on the dildo.

"No," Jenni said. "Never have."

Marsha rubbed lube on the dildo and had Jenni get on her back. Marsha lay on top of Jenni and Jenni guided the dildo to her pussy. Marsha kissed Jenni as she pushed the dildo into her. Jenni was tight, so Marsha had to rock her hips back and forth until Jenni's pussy opened up enough for her to get it all the way in.

Jenni hadn't tried a dildo before. She didn't think a dildo could compare with the real thing. But she was wrong. Maybe it was the way Marsha held and kissed her as she slid the hard rubber appendage in and out of her pussy. Jenni realized she had her wife back in her arms and the love that she had for Marsha came flowing out of her. She thought that love was gone, dead and buried when they signed the divorce papers, but here it was back in full force.

She wrapped her legs around Marsha's waist as Marsha drove the dildo in and out of her. Jenni began to whimper as she felt her muscles tightening. Her nipples ached, and her stomach was full of butterflies.

"If you keep doing that, I'm going to come," Jenni said.

Marsha smiled at Jenni before licking her nipples.

"I have no intention of stopping," Marsha said.

Marsha pushed into Jenni harder. Jenni lifted her ass to meet Marsha's thrusts. She squeezed her eyes shut as her orgasm ripped through her. She groaned loudly as her body convulsed.

Marsha slowed down but didn't pull out. Multiple mini-orgasms exploded in Jenni. She thought she'd never stop coming.

Finally, Marsha pulled out and curled up next to Jenni.

"That was so much fun," Marsha said.

"It sure was," Jenni agreed. "But now it's my turn to wear the strap-on."

Chapter Seven

The chlorine in the pool stung Jenni's nose, but she dived into the water anyway. She sliced through the water while kicking her feet. She never swam now without a swim cap, swim goggles, and a nose plug. Once in the pool, the world faded away and Jenni was alone with her thoughts.

Jenni was pleased that she had accomplished two important things before she left Marsha's house. First, she got the money from Marsha for her services plus a generous tip. And second, before Marsha paid her, Jenni had used the strap-on to fuck Marsha to six screaming orgasms. Jenni had wanted to get her to have lucky number seven orgasm, but Marsha begged Jenni to stop before she completely lost her mind.

What they did last night wasn't just sex. Jenni wasn't just an escort doing her job. It was making love. Jenni could feel it and she was sure Marsha felt it too. There were moments when wearing the strap-on let Jenni imagine that she was Johnny again making love to his wife, Marsha. Johnny was never able to make Marsha have multiple orgasms like she did last night. He never knew how. But Jenni knew how to because she had a vagina.

Once Jenni became Johnny again, he'd know better how to make love to a woman. He'd know what a woman needed. Not just for sex but for everything. Johnny would know how to make Marsha happy.

Jenni stopped swimming in mid-lap. She was in the deep end and had to stand on the tips of her toes to keep her head above water.

Did Johnny really want Marsha back? Or was it Jenni who wanted Marsha? Make it simple. The person in the pool at that moment wanted Marsha and would find a way to get her.

Jenni finished her laps as if she were racing toward a finish line.

Chapter Eight

When Jenni returned to her room, she found Mr. Jones waiting for her.

Mr. Jones ran the casino. The casino was more than just a gaudy building filled with slot machines, black jack tables, roulette wheels, and endless buffets. The casino was a company that owned a lot of things in Las Vegas. One of the things the casino owned was Jenni.

Jenni stood before Mr. Jones, still wet from her swim in the pool. Water dripped off her and formed a puddle at her feet.

"You've been living here for a while," Mr. Jones said as he glanced around the small motel room.

"It's been a few months," Jenni said.

She knew exactly how long she'd been trapped here, but she wasn't going to say it. He knew it as well.

"It looks like you just moved in," Mr. Jones said. "I'm surprised you didn't add some pictures or something. Anything. It could really use a woman's touch."

"No need for that," Jenni said. "I don't plan to be here that long."

Mr. Jones smiled and nodded.

"You always were a good hustler," he said. "You've been busting your ass and it's paid off. You've shaved at least a year off your debt."

"Do you mind if I get out of this wet swimsuit? I'm freezing my ass off."

"Sure. Go ahead."

Jenni went into the bathroom and peeled off the one-piece swimsuit. She hung it up to dry. She toweled off her body and rubbed some warmth back into her limbs. It wasn't just the air conditioning that had chilled her to the bone.

She walked into the room. She didn't care that Mr. Jones saw her naked. The casino owned her so in a very real sense he owned her. He could see his property.

"Just one year?" Jenni said. "I thought I'd paid off more than that."

She opened the top drawer of the dresser and took out a pair of panties and a bra. She stepped into the panties and pulled them up. Then she put on the bra. She could feel Mr. Jones watching her.

"No," he said. "Just a year. But considering the amount you owe, that's still very impressive."

"Thanks," Jenni said.

She opened the bottom drawer. She selected a pair of gray yoga pants and tossed them on the bed.

"How would you like to erase the full debt?" Mr. Jones said.

Jenni froze.

The room wobbled, or she wobbled, she wasn't sure which. She sat down on the edge of the bed.

"I would like that," Jenni said. "What do I have to do?"

She knew he wasn't propositioning her. If he was interested in sex, he could have any woman he wanted. Or any gender swap gambler that tickled his fancy. And he could get it for a hell of a lot less than what Jenni owed the casino.

"I want you what you do best," Mr. Jones said. "I want you to play poker."

Jenni's shoulder slumped.

"I can't do that," she said. "That's gambling. It's against the rules."

"Yes. But I made the rules. If I tell you to gamble, then you're not breaking the rules."

"Viktor showed me what happens to people who break the rules."

Mr. Jones groaned.

"That Russian prick," he said. "Most of the time, he's a good employee. But every so often he does something stupid. I suspect his mother drank too much Vodka before he was born."

Jenni dragged the blanket off the bed and wrapped it around her like a shroud.

"I couldn't snitch on Brittany," she said. "She was my best friend."

Mr. Jones crossed his legs.

"We didn't expect you to," he said. "You weren't the only one who didn't tell us what Brittany was doing. Viktor decided to take you out to the desert on his own. I didn't tell him to."

"Why?" Jenni said.

"I can't say for sure, but my guess is that it's because of that legendary cool of yours. People like Viktor want to see if they can make you fall apart. But you didn't fall apart. You kept your cool. That's partly why I want you to play poker for me."

Jenni narrowed her eyes at Mr. Jones.

"There are better poker players than me at your disposal. Half the gender swap gamblers living at this motel are more skilled than me," she said.

365

"Don't sell yourself short, Jenni," Mr. Jones said. "They might be more skilled, but you're the best. I need you to play for me."

Jenni let the blanket slide off her shoulders.

"And if I do play poker," she said, "then you'll erase my debt?"

Mr. Jones smiled.

"That's right," he said.

"And you'll give me my cock back?"

"Every inch of it. Do we have a deal?"

Jenni took a deep breath.

"Yes," she said. "We have a deal."

"Now, there's just one catch," Mr. Jones said.

There was always a catch.

"What's that?" Jenni said.

"You have to win."

Chapter Nine

Most people would not have been able to sleep. Knowing that they were going to have to do something that their very life depended on would make it impossible for most people to get any shuteye.

But Jenni wasn't most people.

As Johnny, she'd been in too many of high stakes games. When Mr. Jones offered Jenni a way to get her cock back by playing a do or die poker game, instead of making her nervous, it had the opposite effect. This was the calmest she'd been in weeks. She was going to play poker, the thing she loved to do more than just about anything else. She had a big game to play. Nothing was more fun than a big game. The bigger the better.

Part of playing a big game was the preparation. Johnny had developed a ritual, which Jenni followed now. She picked out the clothes she would wear to the game. She did finger exercises. And then, she went to bed and fell into a deep sleep.

She had no dreams.

When she woke up, she felt refreshed. She took a shower. She was about to get dressed when someone knocked on the door. She glanced at the bedside clock. Mr. Jones wasn't having her picked up for the game for hours. She answered the door. It was Lucy.

"Hey girlfriend," Lucy said. "Let's grab something to eat."

"I can't," Jenni said. "I have to get ready for work. I have a special client tonight."

"Wear the red lingerie. You know the outfit I'm talking about."

"What? The red corset with matching panties and garter belt?"

"That's the one."

"Why?"

"You look really hot in that outfit. If you say this client is special, then make it special."

"Maybe I will."

"Hey, don't forget about tomorrow."

The next night was the gender swap gamblers' night off. All the gamblers would get together to play poker for Tic Tacs. Jenni didn't dare tell Lucy that she wouldn't be joining them.

"I won't," Jenni said. "See you tomorrow."

Jenni closed the door. She went to the dresser and took out the red corset. She held it over her chest and looked at herself in the mirror. She hadn't planned on wearing anything sexy. It was too distracting, and she had no idea who she would be playing against. But she might need to create a distraction.

Two hours later, there was another knock at the door. Logan was at the door.

"You ready to go?" he said.

"I'm ready," Jenni said.

She wore a burgundy tracksuit and pink tennis shoes. The zipper for the tracksuit's hoodie was pulled all the way up to her neck and the hood was pulled over her head. Even though the sun had gone down, she wore mirrored sunglasses. She climbed into the backseat and stared at the floorboard. Logan got in and glanced in the rear-view mirror at her.

"That perfume you're wearing," he said.

"What about it?" Jenni said.

"I like it. It's really nice. I mean, you smell fantastic."

Jenni rewarded his compliment with a half-smile.

"Thanks," she said.

Logan drove out of the parking lot and soon they were on the freeway.

"I know what you're doing," Logan said. "Back when had a pussy I used to do the

370

same thing. I'd have a big game against some top-notch players. I'd use any advantage I could think of. I would wear a really nice perfume. Nothing too strong. Just enough. It's the little distractions that work the best."

Jenni leaned forward and rested her arms on the front seat.

"You know about the poker game?" she said.

Logan nodded.

"Yeah," he said. "But that's all I know. Mr. Jones is having you play poker. I don't know why or who you're playing. That info is apparently above my pay grade."

Jenni sat back in her seat.

"It doesn't matter," she said. "Only the game matters."

Chapter Ten

Keith and Bruno were waiting for Jenni when she arrived at the casino. They flanked her as they led her through the casino. They stopped outside a door with a Staff Only sign. Keith used his security card to unlock it. They went through and made their way through the casino's hidden corridors to the door of Mr. Jones' spacious office.

Bruno knocked on the door. They heard Mr. Jones tell them to come in. Keith opened the door. He held it open until Jenni entered and then closed it without coming with her. She stood alone in front of Mr. Jones enormous desk. Behind him were three rows of security camera monitors. Mr. Jones rose and came around to her.

"You look like you're ready to play some poker," he said.

"I'm ready to win," Jenni said.

Mr. Jones laughed.

"That's my girl." He reached into his jacket and produced an overloaded envelope. He handed her the envelope. "Here. This should get you started. I'll get you more if you need it."

Jenni opened the envelope. It was stuffed with bills. Most were twenties, but there were some fifties and a few hundred dollar bills as well. She put the envelope in her pink purse.

"Should be all I need," she said.

Mr. Jones grinned.

"Getting a pussy didn't make you stupid or make you lose your cool," he said.

"No sir," she said. "It didn't."

"Good. Come with me."

They left the office. Bruno and Keith were nowhere in sight. Mr. Jones led her to a service elevator that required a key to access. Mr. Jones fished a key ring out of his pocket, selected a key, and summoned the elevator. As they waited for the elevator to arrive, Jenni thought about how Johnny and

Mr. Jones were the same height. But he towered over Jenni. Along with her cock, she would also get her height back.

The elevator arrived, and they got on. Mr. Jones pressed the button for the twentieth floor. Jenni's stomach clinched tightly. The room where she'd lost the last of her money was on the twentieth floor.

She took a deep breath and calmed herself down. That floor had four private poker rooms. It was where exclusive games were played away from prying eyes. Of course, the game would be held in one of those four rooms. It didn't matter if tonight's game was in the same room where she lost her gender. She was determined to win it back.

"You'll be playing with five men," Mr. Jones said. "Two of them are generals. Two are defense contractor representatives. The fifth man is a senator on the Armed Services Committee. I need you to beat all of them. The defense reps and the senator should be easy. They're not very good. But the generals are good players. Play them as if this were a professional circuit game."

"Without mercy," Jenni said.

"Exactly."

"I take it they all know each other."

"Yes. They do."

"What did you tell them about me?"

Mr. Jones peered down at Jenni and grinned.

"You're my niece, Jenni Jones," he said. "You're a spoiled rich girl who thinks she's a big-time gambler. You only want to play with high rollers and asked me to find you a game."

Jenni rolled her eyes. If she had known she was going to play a rich bitch, she would have worn more make-up and some jewelry.

"What did they say when you told them that?" she said.

"They said they wanted to meet you first and then they'd decide if you could join them."

Jenni pulled down the zipper to her hoodie until she was showing a generous amount of cleavage.

"Maybe this will help them decide," she said.

The elevator reached the twentieth floor. Mr. Jones led the way to the poker room. To Jenni's relief, it wasn't the same one where she lost her gender.

"A few more thing before we go in," Mr. Jones said. "The security cameras for these rooms can only be seen in my office. I'll be watching the entire time."

Jenni nodded.

"Okay," she said.

"Did you bring your phone? The one you use to communicate with Logan?"

Jenni opened her purse, took out the phone, and held it up.

"Right here."

"Good. I might need to call you."

Mr. Jones knocked and entered without waiting for a reply. Jenni followed him in. The poker table was in the center of the elegantly decorated room, but no one was sitting at the table. The five men were loitering about the room, making drinks at the stocked bar or reclining on one of the couches. When they saw Mr. Jones, they gathered around him.

He introduced them to Jenni. She gave them all a big smile and shook their hands when Mr. Jones told her their names. When he got to the last man, Jenni hesitated before shaking his hand. They had met before. It was Holt Cooper.

If he recognized her as the escort he had screwed for hours a few days earlier, he didn't show it. Jenni also showed no sign that she knew him.

"What do you say, boys?" Jenni said, thrusting out her chest. "Can I play with you?"

The men busted out laughing.

"We're talking playing cards, right?" said the senator.

"That's right," Jenni said.

"Darn!"

The men laughed again. Jenni joined them.

"Sure," the senator said, speaking for all of them. "We would be delighted to have you join us."

He put his arm around Jenni's shoulder and escorted her to the table. One of the contractors asked her if she wanted something to drink. Jenni asked if they had a decent white wine. Mr. Jones assured her that the bar had an excellent selection of wine. He gave Jenni a peck on the top of her head and told the men to take good care of his niece. And then he left the room.

Once everyone had a drink and were settled in at the table, Holt broke the seal on a fresh pack of cards. Everyone anted up, the cards were dealt, and the game began.

Chapter Eleven

The Senator was the first player who busted. He was more bluster than skill. Jenni figured he was playing with taxpayers' money so the sooner he was out the better.

The other players were shocked at how well Jenni played. The contractors didn't seem to care that they were losing to a girl, they just hated losing. But she could tell that it really irked the generals that a female was winning most of the hands.

The general who wasn't Holt was so annoyed at the pile of money in front of Jenni, that he got sloppy trying to win his money back from her. He made foolish bluffs, none of which paid off. He was the second player who busted.

Holt looked around the table at the remaining players and then studied his watch.

"We've been playing for five hours," he said.

"I'm doing fine," one of the contractors said.

"I want a chance to win my money back," the other contractor said.

"I was just going to suggest that we take a break," Holt said.

"That's a good idea," Jenni said. "I've been needing to pee for about an hour."

Everyone got up and stretched. The senator and the general took the opportunity to say good night and left the room. The senator made a point of hugging Jenni goodbye and coping a feel of her tit. Jenni made a mental note to never vote for that asshole.

The poker rooms had their own private bathrooms, one for men and the other for women. Jenni dashed into the women's room and got to a toilet before she wet herself. She sighed as she emptied her full bladder. Then she washed up before going back out.

Holt was waiting for her outside the bathroom door.

"You're a damn good player," he said.

"Thank you," Jenni said. "So are you."

"Have we met somewhere before?"

Jenni squinted at the ceiling as if she were trying to remember.

"Have you ever been to Cabo?" she said. "You remind me of a guy I met on the beach."

Holt grinned.

"Sorry. Never been there."

"You should go. The beach is divine."

Jenni hurried back to the table before he could ask any more questions. The game continued. It was almost dawn before the two contractors ran out of money. They left the room bleary-eyed but proud that they had lasted as long as they had.

"It's just you and me now," Holt said.

"I don't feel like stopping," Jenni said.

"Neither do I."

The money was split evenly between them. The blinds were shut tightly so they didn't see the sun rise. For Jenni, only the cards existed as they played hand after hand. She knew Holt's tells and anticipated his bluffs. The pile of money in front of him shrank while her pile grew.

Holt was down to his last few dollars when Jenni decided it was time to end the game. She upped the ante beyond what he had. Holt looked down at his pitiful stack of money.

"I don't have enough to cover the bet," he said.

"Then you're done," Jenni said. "The game is over."

"Wait. I can cover the bet, but I need a little time."

Jenni was going to refuse. He was out of money. The game was over. She'd won.

But then, her phone rang. There was only person who would be calling right now. She answered the phone.

"Hello?" she said.

"Let him get what he needs to cover the bet," Mr. Jones said.

"You sure about that?"

"Don't ask questions. Just tell him you'll wait."

Mr. Jones hung up.

"Sure," Jenni said. "I don't have any plans for today. I'd love to keep playing."

Holt sprang from the table, huddled in a corner, and made a phone call. He held his hand over the receiver as he talked. After he hung up, he returned to the table.

"It's on its way," he said.

Jenni didn't ask what the it was. She went to the bar.

"I'm going to make a pot of coffee," she said.

"Bless you," Holt said.

While they waited for the coffee to brew, Holt did push-ups. When the coffee was ready, Jenni poured them both a cup. They both drank their coffee black. They talked about basketball until there was a knock on the door.

Holt answered. It was the soldier who had taken Jenni on a covert mission from the Bellagio to Holt's room in the Four Queens. He handed Holt a metal briefcase. Jenni thought it might be the same one she saw in the safe of Holt's closet.

No sooner had the soldier left the room when Mr. Jones entered. Holt didn't seem surprised by the casino manager's sudden appearance. He handed Holt an envelope of money. Holt kept the briefcase and counted the money.

"It's worth more than this," Holt said.

"I think it's generous," Mr. Jones said.

"Forget it."

"Wait. I'll sweeten the pot. You get this, and you'll have an open tab at the casino for the next year."

"I can play as much as I want, and you'll cover me?"

"That's right."

Holt scratched the stubble on his chin.

"Make it five years," he said.

Mr. Jones growled low in his throat, and then he smiled.

"It's a deal," he said.

He held out his hand.

"One more thing," Holt said. "I keep the briefcase. For now. If I lose what's in this envelope, then you get it. But if I win my money back, then I keep the briefcase and I return what's in this envelope."

Mr. Jones stared at Jenni. Then he turned back to Holt and grinned.

"You drive a hard bargain, General Cooper," he said.

The men shook hands and sealed the deal.

Chapter Twelve

Mr. Jones left the room. Holt sat down at the table and put the briefcase on the floor next to his chair. He took out the money in the envelope and spread it out in a fan. He counted enough to cover the last bet. He glared at Jenni. She glared back.

"Call," Holt said.

Jenni showed her cards. Holt had the better hand. He laughed as he raked in the pot.

"See?" he said. "My luck is already changing."

But his luck didn't change. He won a few hands, but Jenni won more. A lot more. Jenni glanced at her watch. They had played for seventeen hours. That didn't bother Jenni. Holt was a tough player, but she was the seasoned pro.

His pile of money shrank again. They were down to what was potentially Holt's last hand when he asked for a break.

"Good idea," Jenni said. "All that coffee is getting to me."

"Me too," Holt said. "I need to piss like a racehorse."

They went to the bathrooms. Jenni peed for what felt like an hour. When she stepped out of the stall, Holt was in the bathroom waiting for her.

"This is the wrong bathroom," Jenni said. "Men's room is next door."

"We need to talk," Holt said.

Jenni washed her hands and splashed water on her face.

"What about?" Jenni said.

"Drop the bullshit," he said. "You're not Mr. Jones' niece. You're a prostitute and apparently a professional gambler."

Jenni dried her hands and then leaned against the sink.

"Yes, I am," she said. "And you still agreed to let me play."

"What are you talking about?"

"You recognized me the second I walked in. You don't fuck somebody as long as you fucked me and forget their face. You must have suspected that I was a ringer, but you didn't say jack shit."

"I'm saying something now."

"Too late. You had a hundred chances to back out. You didn't because your male ego wouldn't let you. You were determined not to let a girl beat you."

Holt turned on the water and stuck his head in the sink. The water poured over him. He stood and shook his head like a dog, sending water everywhere. Jenni flinched but she couldn't avoid getting splattered.

"You have to let me win," Holt said. "I can't let Mr. Jones get that briefcase."

Jenni narrowed her eyes at Holt.

"What's in it?"

"I can't tell you. It's top secret."

"If it's that fucking valuable, then why did you bring it?"

Holt looked down at the floor.

"I'm addicted to gambling. I can't quit. I keep going even when I know I should stop."

"Shit," Jenni said. "Welcome to the club."

Holt grabbed her arm.

"I should never have brought the briefcase, but I knew how much Mr. Jones wanted it. You have to let me win my money back."

Jenni took Holt's hand off her arm.

"If he wants it that bad," she said, "can you imagine what's going to happen to me if I lose?"

Holt bent down and pulled up his pant leg, revealing a handgun in an ankle holster. He removed a handgun.

"I'll protect you," Holt said. "Let's just get the hell out of here. Right now."

Jenni held up her hands.

"Whoa there, cowboy," she said. "I can't go with you."

"Mr. Jones can't get that fucking briefcase," Holt said as he put the gun back in the holster. "I'm not even supposed to have it. If the Pentagon ever found out I took it, I would be court-martialed. It's bad enough I used the first batch to settle my debts, but this is the last batch. After this, there is no more. I can cover the disappearance of the first batch, but not this one."

Icy fingers raced down Jenni's spine. What Holt was saying was starting to make sense.

"Let me guess," she said. "In the briefcase are doses of nanobots. And these nanobots can change a person's gender. And these are the last doses in existence."

Holt drew back and stared at Jenni.

"Yes," he said. "That's exactly what's in the briefcase."

"Did you know what Mr. Jones has been doing with those nanobots?"

"I've tried not to think about it."

"He takes male gamblers who owe him a lot of money and he turns them into women. Then the women have to work as whores to pay off their debt."

"Holy shit. How do you know all this?"

"I'm one of them! That's right, Holt. You fucked a dude with a pussy."

Holt looked Jenni over and then looked down at his crotch.

"Holy shit."

"Yeah. Holy shit."

"What do we do now?"

"We let the cards decide."

Jenni and Holt returned to the table. Now that they knew the real stakes, a deadly seriousness settled over the table. They were both playing for their lives.

"Are you hot?" Jenni said fanning her face with her hand. "Because I'm really hot. I need to cool down."

She unzipped her hoodie and took it off. Then she slipped off the velour sweatpants. Underneath the tracksuit, she wore the red corset with matching panties and garter belt. She leaned forward so that Holt got an excellent view of her breasts nestled in red lace.

"That's not fair," Holt said.

"Who said poker was fair," Jenni said.

Holt dealt a new hand. He traded in three cards and Jenni traded in two. They anted up. Jenni raised the stakes until everything Holt had was in the pot. He gave away no tells or tried any bluffs. Jenni had no clue what he was holding.

Jenni looked at her cards again. She wasn't happy, but this was the hand that fate had dealt her.

"Call," Jenni said.

Holt had four Jacks and an Ace high. Jenni's eyes filled with tears.

She had four Queens. She had won the game.

Holt jumped to his feet. He snatched the briefcase off the floor and held it against his chest.

"Keep the money," he said. "I'm keeping the briefcase."

Mr. Jones burst into the room with Viktor close behind him.

"You lost fair and square, General Cooper," Mr. Jones said. "Now hand over the briefcase."

"No!" Holt shouted. "I won't."

Mr. Jones nodded at Viktor. Viktor pulled a gun out of his pocket. Holt didn't reach for his gun. He held onto the briefcase instead. Viktor shot Holt in the head. His brains splattered on the wall behind him. Holt slumped to the floor. Jenni screamed and dived under the table. Mr. Jones calmly walked over to Holt's body and pried the briefcase from his fingers.

"I'm sorry it had to end this way, General," Mr. Jones said.

Mr. Jones put the briefcase on the table and popped it open. While he inspected the contents, Jenni crawled over to Holt's body. She couldn't believe he was dead. Viktor and Mr. Jones' attention was on the briefcase, so they didn't notice Jenni remove Holt's gun from the ankle holster and put it in her purse.

Mr. Jones snapped the briefcase shut.

"I have to put this in my safe," he said. "Clean up in here."

Viktor pointed his gun at Mr. Jones.

"Sorry, boss," Viktor said. "But I must take briefcase from you."

Mr. Jones glared at Viktor.

"What the fuck do you think you're doing?"

Viktor shrugged.

"I told my old bosses in Russian mob about nanobots. Russian government will pay lots of money for briefcase and mob will give me my old job back."

"Why would you want to work for the Russian mob when you can work for me?" Mr. Jones said.

"I got kicked out of mob for bad behavior. I miss Russia. I hate Las Vegas. Too hot here. Give me briefcase."

"I'm sure we can work out a deal."

"Sorry. No deal."

Viktor shot Mr. Jones in the chest. Mr. Jones stared at the hole in his chest.

"Fucking asshole," Mr. Jones said.

Those were his last words. Mr. Jones fell to the floor. His blood soaked the expensive carpet.

Viktor sauntered over to the table and picked up the briefcase. He bent over and pointed the gun at Jenni.

"Come out little girl," he said.

Jenni quivered heavily as she climbed to her feet.

"What are you going to do to me?" she asked.

"I must take you to pit after all," Viktor said.

"Why?"

"I can't leave witnesses."

"Who would fucking believe me?"

Viktor squinted at the ceiling.

"Probably nobody, but I can't take that chance."

"I'll make a deal with you," Jenni said.

"Everybody want to make deal with me."

"You'll like this one."

Viktor sat at the table. He held his gun loosely in his hand.

"Okay. Let's hear it."

"I'll give you a blow job."

"That's it?"

"No. If I made you come in less than five minutes, then you let me live. If I don't..."

"I put bullet in your head."

Jenni gulped.

"Exactly. Do we have a deal?"

Viktor stood and unzipped his fly. "You got deal."

Chapter Thirteen

Jenni chose a spot on the floor where she wouldn't get blood on her knees. The smell of blood hung in the air. She could taste in the back of her throat. It tasted like iron.

She placed her pink purse between her knees. Viktor stood over her and grinned down at her. His cock hung out of his fly. He was already erect. He apparently got sexually aroused from killing people.

"Don't forget that I have gun in my hand," Viktor said. "You try to bite me or run away or do anything stupid, I shoot you. Understand?"

Jenni nodded.

"I understand."

She reached for his belt, but he put his hand on her head.

"Wait," Viktor said. "I need to time you. Make me come in five minutes or I kill you. That's the deal, right?"

"Right," Jenni said.

Viktor took a step back. He put his gun in his back pocket and fiddled with his watch. When he was done, he showed her the watch.

"My watch has an alarm," he said. "I've set for five minutes from now."

"Then I'd better get started," Jenni said.

"This is an excellent watch. You want to know where I got it?"

"Tell me later."

Viktor shrugged. He took the gun out of his back pocket and stepped toward Jenni. She unbuckled his belt and unbuttoned his jeans. She pulled his jeans down to his knees. He wasn't wearing underwear.

She licked the head of his cock. The salty taste of his pre-come joined the taste of iron in her mouth. She licked the length of his shaft before putting him into her mouth. As she sucked on his cock, she kept her eyes on him.

Viktor gazed back at her until she started playing with his balls. He closed his eyes and moaned with pleasure. As soon as he closed his eyes, Jenni reached down between her legs with her other hand and opened her purse.

She concentrated on sucking on the head of Viktor's cock while stroking his saliva-coated shaft. He rewarded her with more moans. He put his free hand on the top of her head and pushed his cock deeper into her mouth.

While he face-fucked her, Jenni's hands were free to reach into her purse and feel Holt's gun with her fingers. She found the safety latch and flipped it off. She didn't dare cock the gun yet. She was afraid that the click would alert Viktor.

"Being woman has been good for you," Viktor said. "You're much better cocksucker than a gambler. Maybe I let you live, take you to Russia, and make you my number one bitch. Would you like that?"

Jenni didn't answer. She stretched her mouth open, so he could thrust in and out of her. Drool dripped off her chin.

Viktor opened his eyes and checked his watch. He smiled and closed his eyes again.

"Only have two minutes left," he said. "I'm nowhere near done."

Jenni wasn't thinking about the five minutes. It didn't matter if she made him come or not. She knew he planned to kill her no matter what. She only came up with the five-minute blow job as a way to buy time. Time enough to get Holt's gun ready.

But she did plan to make Viktor come in less than five minutes. That part was easy. It wasn't because she was such a great cocksucker, though she had learned to be pretty damn good at it. Back when Johnny played cards with Viktor, he would yammer on and on about how amazing he was in bed. He claimed he could fuck for hours and that after sex with him, women worshipped him and begged him for more. But then right after he bragged about how great he was in bed, he would turn around and tell an embarrassing story like how a hooker once made him squirt the second she put his cock in her mouth by sticking her thumb up his ass.

Jenni snaked her hand between Viktor's legs. She massaged his ass as she slobbered on his cock. And then, she jammed her thumb into his asshole.

Viktor screamed something in Russian. His legs shuddered, and his cock erupted. He groaned like a wounded bull as his sperm filled Jenni's mouth. He was still in the throes of his orgasm when Jenni pulled away, grabbed the jeans bunched around his ankles, and yanked them as hard as she could. Viktor's arms flailed as he tried to keep his balance. His cock was still shooting reams of spunk as he toppled to the floor.

He landed on his back and his head bounced off the carpeting. The impact forced him to drop his gun and it slid across the floor. He sat up and felt the back of his head.

"What the fuck?" Viktor said.

"Don't move," Jenni said.

Jenni stood a few feet away from him. She had Holt's gun in her hands and was pointing it at Viktor's chest.

"Stupid cunt," Viktor said. "You don't have nerve to put bullet in my head."

"I'm not aiming for your head," Jenni said. "It's too small a target."

Jenni fired three times into Viktor's chest. Maybe she didn't need to shoot him three times, but she had to be sure. He certainly looked dead.

Viktor's watch alarm started buzzing, which reminded Jenni that she had to get the fuck out of there quickly. Sooner or later someone was going to come in here looking for one of these people. Jenni had to be gone before they showed up.

She checked her body. Viktor's blood had splattered on her legs. She snatched her velour sweatpants off the chair where she'd left it and used it to wipe the blood off her legs. She went to the bar and found a box of trash bags. She took a bag and stuffed her tracksuit inside it. She went to the table and gathered the pile of money in the center. It was a lot of money. She had earned it. She put the money into the trash bag.

Jenni stared at the briefcase on the table. She fumbled with the latch before getting it open. Three men had died in this room for what was inside. She had been willing to die for it too. She closed the briefcase and put it in the trash bag.

The last thing she put into the bag was Holt's gun.

Clutching the trash bag tightly, Jenni peeked out the door. The hallway was empty. She dashed to the elevator. She was about to push the button when she changed her mind and decided to take the stairs instead. Just as she got inside the stairwell, she heard the elevator ding. She didn't wait to see who was getting off on this floor.

Jenni rushed down the twenty flights of stairs, her heart beating in her ears on every step. Rather than go through the lobby, she went out the service entrance which led to a back alley. She passed two busboys on a smoke break. They barely acknowledged her existence. And then she was on the street.

As she joined the mass of tourists strolling on the sideway, Jenni chuckled even though she was scared shitless. She laughed because here she was, a woman wearing red lingerie and carrying a trash bag walking on a city sidewalk on a late weekday afternoon. In any other city, she would have turned heads and been stared at. But this was Las Vegas. She didn't stand out at all here.

Jenni stood on a corner and hailed a taxi. The first two cabs went right by here but the third stopped and she hopped in. Slamming the door shut, she leaned back and took her first full breath.

"Where to?" the cabbie said.

Jenni's brow knitted as she considered her next move. There were a million places she'd rather be than in Vegas at that moment, but she knew where she had to go.

"The Moonbeam Motor Lodge," she said.

Chapter Fourteen

Jenni entered room thirteen and rifled through the dresser drawers. She grabbed just enough clothes to keep her going for a few days. She took Johnny's T-shirt and hoodie out of the bottom drawer and added them to the pile. She put everything into the trash bag.

There wasn't time to make long term plans and she needed to travel lightly. She stripped off the red corset with the matching panties and garter belt. She couldn't stand to have them on her body for another minute. The red reminded her of all the blood she'd seen that day. She put on a plain white bra and panties, jeans, and a sweatshirt.

She peeked out the curtain. As usual, the parking lot was empty. With the trash bag in hand, Jenni walked past the pool to room thirty-nine. After the casino had Brittany killed, they gave her room and her maid job to Eva. There was no question that the monthly poker game would keep going regardless of who was living in room thirty-nine. The game was too important.

Jenni knocked on the door. Nadia answered.

"We were wondering if you were going to show up," she said. "Come in. Grab some Tic Tacs and a beer and join the game."

"I can't," Jenni said. "I don't have time. In fact, none of us do."

Nadia narrowed her eyes at Jenni.

"What has happened?"

"Let me tell everybody at the same time."

Jenni walked over to the oval table where Clarissa, Sheila, Eva, and Lucy were playing poker. They glanced up at her and smiled or waved hello.

"Mr. Jones is dead," Jenni said.

The women stopped playing poker and stared at Jenni.

"Dead?" Clarissa said. "What do you mean dead?"

"Viktor shot him," Jenni said.

"Why?" Nadia said.

Jenni rummaged inside the trash bag and pulled out the briefcase. She placed it in the middle of the table.

"For this," she said. "Viktor was going to give it to the Russian mob to get his old job back."

"What happened to Viktor?" Lucy said.

"I killed him," Jenni said. "I had to. He was going to kill me."

"What's in the briefcase?" Sheila said.

Jenni opened the briefcase. Inside were four vials filled with clear liquid and four syringes.

"Four queens," Jenni whispered.

"What did you say?" Sheila said.

"Nothing. This is the last batch of the nanobots. There is no more after this."

"But even if we took it," Clarissa said. "We'd still be in debt to the casino."

"Other than Peter, I seriously doubt anyone other than Mr. Jones knew how much we owed the casino," Jenni said. "Peter has enough problems dealing with a dead boss. Which means, our debt has been wiped clean."

"Besides," Eva said as she beamed at the vials. "Our gender was the collateral the casino had to ensure we'd pay our debt. If we get our gender back, then they got nothing on us."

"There's only four vials," Clarissa said. "And six of us."

"Two of us have to stay women," Jenni said. "I'm sorry, but that's how it goes."

The gender swap gamblers gazed at each other.

Lucy put her hands on her hips.

"You can count me out," she said.

The women stared at Lucy. She shrugged her shoulders.

"The truth is," Lucy said. "I paid off my debt last year. That's why I don't see clients anymore. Mr. Jones let me stick around and play den mother to you bitches."

"I don't get it," Eva said. "Why would you choose to keep a pussy when you can have your dick back?"

Lucy grinned and tossed her hair.

"Look at me," she said. "I'm a hot piece of ass. As a man, I was mediocre at best. But as a woman, I'm sexy as shit. I know looks don't last forever and there are disadvantages to being a woman, but it wasn't like my life as a man was all that great. I like being a chick. And I get a hell of lot more pussy now than I did as a man."

Jenni turned to the others.

"Okay," she said. "That leaves five of us."

"You can count me out too," Nadia said.

"Now I'm really shocked," Sheila said. "You're one of the most badass men I've ever known."

Nadia sighed.

"True. I was a badass, a mean motherfucker, and a terrible man. I know women can be ruthless bitches, but I'm a much better person as a woman than I ever was a man. I like myself better this way."

Jenni looked at the other three women.

"Anyone else want to stay a woman?" she asked.

Clarissa stood.

"Fuck no," she said. "I want my damn dick back."

"Me too," Eva said.

"Me three," Sheila said.

The three women removed their clothes. Jenni injected Eva first. The woman watched in amazement as her body convulsed and changed until Eva was Ernesto. When the pain of transformation subsided, he jumped out of his chair and grabbed his cock.

"Thank Jesus!" he shouted. "You're back. How I missed you. I'm going to my room to jerk off right now."

Ernesto rushed out of the room.

Clarissa was next. She had told Jenni that Colin had a big cock and he didn't lie. Though Jenni was sorry to say goodbye to Clarissa's big boobs and wide ass.

Colin pulled Jenni aside.

"If for some reason you decide not to change back," he said. "Come see me."

Jenni didn't respond.

She gave Sheila her injection. As far as Jenni was concerned, this was a real shame. Sheila was a hot Jewish mama, but Stu was a skinny guy with a hairy back and knobby knees. Still, he was extremely happy until he noticed that for some reason, when he transformed back, his cock came back uncircumcised.

"You mean I have to get another bris?" Stu said.

"Stop bitching," Colin said. "An hour ago, you didn't have a foreskin."

"Good point."

414

"That leaves you, Jenni," Lucy said. "Do you want me to give you the injection."

"No," Jenni said. "I'll do it myself."

"What are you waiting for? You've been hustling harder than any of us to get your cock back. Inject yourself and be Johnny again."

Jenni looked into the briefcase. There was one vial and one syringe left. She closed the briefcase.

"Not yet," Jenni said. "There are some things I need to think about first."

Chapter Fifteen

Marsha was in the kitchen doing the dishes. She hated washing one set of dishes. It was a reminder that she was alone. Things didn't work out like she had expected with Keith. With Keith out of the way, memories of Johnny had crept back into her mind. She didn't understand why she couldn't forget that guy. She also kept thinking about Jenni. Johnny and Jenni. They were so different, yet they were alike in that they had both made her feel special. She thought about calling the escort agency and asking for Jenni. But she wasn't in the mood for sex right now.

Marsha was deep in thought and didn't hear the cab stop in front of her house. She jumped when she heard the doorbell. She dried her hands with a dishtowel and answered the door. She smiled when she saw who it was.

"Hey," Marsha said. "I didn't expect to see you."

"Is it okay that I'm here?"

"Yeah. In fact, I've been thinking about you lately."

"Good things I hope."

"Yeah. Come on in."

"Actually, can I stay here with you?"

Marsha thought it over.

"Sure," she said. "That would be nice. How long are you planning on staying?"

"As long as you let me."

"Well, let's take it one day at a time and see how it goes."

"That works for me."

"By the way. What's in the briefcase?"

The End

www.ingramcontent.com/pod-product-compliance
Lightning Source LLC
Chambersburg PA
CBHW070351260626
4716ICB00001B/100